Secrets in the Park

A Secret Identity novella

By Helen Gray

Copyright © **2017**
Written by: Helen Gray
Published by: Forget Me Not Romances, a division of Winged Publications

This book is a work of fiction. Names, characters, places, and incidents are the product of the author's imagination and are used fictitiously. Any resemblance to actual events, locales, or persons, living or dead, is coincidental

All rights reserved

1. Scriptures taken from the Holy Bible, New International Version®, NIV®. Copyright © 1973, 1978, 1984, 2011 by Biblica, Inc.™ Used by permission of Zondervan. All rights reserved worldwide. www.zondervan.com The "NIV" and "New International Version" are trademarks registered in the United States Patent and Trademark Office by Biblica, Inc.™
2. Scripture quotations marked (NIV) are taken from the Holy Bible, New International Version®, NIV®. Copyright © 1973, 1978, 1984, 2011 by Biblica, Inc.™ Used by permission of Zondervan. All rights reserved worldwide. www.zondervan.com The "NIV" and "New International Version" are trademarks registered in the United States Patent and Trademark Office by Biblica, Inc.™

All rights reserved.

ISBN-10:1-946939-01-3
ISBN-13:978-1-946939-01-2

"Secret Identity (1/5)

For there is nothing hidden that will not be disclosed, and nothing concealed that will not be known or brought out into the open. Luke 8:17 (NIV)

Chapter 1

Jan Blevins—the name she was using while here—folded the newspaper she had been reading and placed it on her lap, blinking away tears. She leaned back against the park bench and let her gaze swing over the scene remembered from her childhood.

It was a bright, summery morning in mid-May. Stately magnolia trees formed a border along the lush lawn on this side of Central Avenue where Bathhouse Row, eight bathhouses aligned in a row, resided. The Buckstaff, Fordyce, Hale, Lamar, Maurice, Ozark, Quapaw, and Superior had been built between 1911 and 1923.

Designated a National Historic Landmark in 1987, Hot Springs National Park surrounded the north end of the city and was the smallest national park by area in the United States. Directly across from it, the Central Avenue historic district of Hot Springs, Arkansas, boasted hotels, shops, banks, restaurants, and offices built in a variety of architectural styles. The majority of the buildings were two- or three-story structures. Hot Springs was a thriving city built around the thermal springs for which it was known.

Jan glanced down at the paper on her lap. Jordan Baldwin's face stared up at her, bringing a fresh spate of grief. *We'll find out who killed you, Jordy. I promise. It won't bring you back, but it'll bring justice and clear your name.*

Jan's earliest memories were of playing with Jordan and his sister in their backyards. Her dad had worked for Lyle Baldwin, and the two families had spent a lot of time together.

Then, when she was nine and her brother ten, their parents had divorced, and their mother had taken Jan and Brodie back to her hometown of Evansville, Indiana, with her to live near her parents. Mother had remarried a year later and refused to take Jan and Brodie back to Hot Springs to visit their dad. The only time they had seen him had been when he made the trip to Indiana and claimed them for weekends that they spent visiting area places of interest to Jan and her brother—and sleeping in hotels.

Jan and Brodie had looked forward to those weekends and reveled in them. Jan's plan growing up had been to move back to Hot Springs after she graduated from high school, but those plans had been abandoned when they received word that her dad had died of a heart attack. She had been fifteen at the time.

When Lyle Baldwin called last week and asked for her help, Jan had left her CPA office in her assistant's care, and come. Already grief stricken over Jordy's death and Lyle's grief, she had welcomed the opportunity, agreed to alter her name, concocted a cover story for her presence in the area, and arranged to stay here long enough to help Lyle search for answers.

Jan started to rise from the park bench, but movement and sound from up the street made her pause. A motorized wheelchair rolled erratically down the sidewalk toward her, the driver yodeling drunkenly at the top of his lungs. Suddenly the chair swerved in at the Fordyce entrance. Then it veered off the walkway onto the lawn and rolled around and around in a crazy version of a 'wheelchair wheelie.' It was a comical sight, yet disturbing. Suddenly the driver steered out of the circular pattern and picked up speed. He raced forward, still yodeling, and ran smack into a tree. The chair tipped over, and the man pitched forward.

Again Jan started to rise, but the sound of running feet echoed behind her. A park ranger ran past her, so close he nearly stepped on her toes. She tucked her feet further beneath the bench and watched as the ranger reached the wrecked chair and dropped to his knees next to the dislodged driver. He began to check the man for injuries.

Behind her a siren sounded, and a police car pulled to the curb and slid to a stop. An officer emerged and ran to join the pair on the lawn.

After some discussion, the police officer righted the wheelchair, and the ranger helped the driver sit upright. Together they placed the man back in his chariot.

When the man said something—apparently something rude—the officer pulled a ticket booklet from his pocket and flipped it open. He wrote for several moments, tore out a leaf, and handed it to the driver.

When the cop moved behind the chair and pushed it across the lawn to his car, the ranger turned and headed back toward where Jan had sat, bemused, through the scenario.

Had the cop just given a wheelchair driver a ticket and arrested him? She snickered at the thought and raised the newspaper from her lap to cover her face. Her eyes closed as laughter made her torso quiver.

"Are you all right, Ma'am?"

~

Kyler watched the young woman lower the newspaper enough to reveal huge, shiny dark eyes. The huffing noise and body shakes stopped.

Impulsively he scooted onto the bench next to her. "You can come out now. They're gone."

She lowered the paper, and her expression became solemn in a face that was easy on the eyes—incredibly so. Heavy dark hair swirled around it and spilled to her shoulders. She was nicely built, too, probably about five four or five, with nice laugh lines at the corners of her wide mouth. He estimated her to be a year or two younger than his thirty.

He grinned. "You think it's funny that the guy was given a DWI for driving a wheelchair while intoxicated?"

Her head bobbed, and a sound resembling a snort came from her. "I never heard of such a thing." She glanced over at the police car. "Where did they go?"

"To the police station. It's faster and easier to push Boomer—I think his real name is Charlie—there than try to get his chair in the car. It's far from his first offense," he explained.

She gave a nod of understanding. "Surely he's not dangerous."

"He is to others. When he goes on a bender, he's apt to drive right out into traffic. He has to be taken off the streets, at least until he's sober."

Kyler's eyes gravitated to the newspaper she had lowered to her lap, and noted the picture and story now visible. He studied her—and where she had chosen to sit. All traces of humor had disappeared from her expression, to be replaced by a look of utter sadness. "Do you have a special interest in that story?"

She gazed past him. "I thought it was interesting."

"Are you aware that you're sitting in the very spot where the man's body was found?"

She drew a deep breath. Then she seemed to gather her thoughts, and met his gaze. "I realized that as I was reading. Maybe it's why the story touched me so much. It was an eerie feeling. Do you know if the police have any idea who killed the man?"

"We're working on the case together, but I'm not at liberty to discuss it."

Her head tilted, and her eyes became slits. "You're working on the case?"

"You bet. The victim was a casual friend, and he was killed on my turf." *And I'd love to be the one to catch the rat who did it.*

"I thought park rangers protected park resources and looked after the tourists."

"We also work to prevent criminal acts within the parks. A percentage of us have degrees in criminal justice and relevant work experience."

A slight lift of her eyebrows indicated a boost in respect. "I'm glad to hear that."

"Are you from around here?" Something told him she was more interested in Jordan Baldwin's death than she was admitting.

"I've just moved here in preparation for starting a new job at the end of the summer."

"And what would that be?"

"I've been contracted to teach business classes at the high school."

His muscles relaxed a bit. She looked the part. Wearing a professional black business dress and matching strappy heels, she looked as if she had just come from, or was going to, a meeting at the school. "What is your name?"

She hesitated a moment, but then seemed to decide that giving a man in uniform her name was safe enough. "Jan Blevins." She stuck out a hand. "And you?"

He grasped the hand briefly and released it. "Kyler Winston. Welcome to Hot Springs, Miss Blevins. I assume it's Miss," he added, glancing at her ringless fingers and struggling to keep his voice calm and impersonal.

"Yes," she said simply, and glanced at her watch. She made a little startled reaction.

"Do you have an appointment?"

"Yes," she said, rising to her feet. "I hope you find that man's killer."

He watched her walk away.

~

Jan turned her silver Camaro into an empty space in the parking lot of the Mid-south Community Bank just after eleven o'clock. She sat for several moments, staring at the modern brick structure where Jordy had worked. A flag fluttered from a flagpole near the entrance.

She rubbed her palms over the top of the steering wheel, her thoughts spinning. In the midst of the questions and possibilities, the park ranger's face intruded. There had been something intriguing about the man. She couldn't put her finger on why. Lean, with dark hair, wary brown eyes and a five o'clock shadow, from the top of his olive green campaign hat to the soles of his lace-up boots, he had been one impressive park ranger.

Jan shook off the fanciful reflections, opened the vehicle door, and headed toward the front entrance. Inside the building, she absorbed her surroundings in a visual sweep as she examined the place where Jordan had been the marketing officer. She wasn't sure what she hoped to accomplish, but she wanted to learn all she could about her childhood playmate's friends and associates. She had to look for answers anywhere and everywhere she could.

Four desks occupied strategic positions in the lobby. To her left were doors labeled Trust and Loan Offices. Directly across the lobby was a large plate glassed office labeled Operations Manager. Inside, two men were engaged in what looked to be a heated exchange.

"May I help you?" a woman asked as Jan approached the first desk.

"My name is Jan Blevins, and I'm looking for supplementary materials for the business classes I'll be teaching at the high school this next term. Do you have someone who can help me?"

The young woman smiled. "It sounds like our marketing director might be a good person to ask. Let me see if he's in his office." She pushed an intercom button. "There's a Miss Blevins here looking for classroom materials." She paused. "Okay."

She replaced the receiver. "He can see you now. His office is the one at the end of the hall on the left." She pointed across the lobby.

Jan walked that way and opened the last door. The man inside looked up from his computer. Dressed in a suit and tie, he was young and blondish, probably not long out of college.

He stood. "Good morning, Miss Blevins. I'm Sean Nichols. What type of materials do you have in mind for your students?"

She put on her fast-thinking cap. "Videos. Pamphlets. Anything that has to do with banking procedures and the necessity of maintaining thorough, accurate financial records."

He adjusted his tie. "I'm not sure what we have on hand, but I'll check and contact you if you'll give me your phone number or email address. I'm new at this job and haven't had time to get fully acquainted with our resources yet."

She feigned surprise. "Oh? Where did you work before coming here?"

"I was with a bank in my hometown of Little Rock. This is an upward move for me."

He seemed pleasant enough, but Jan had to squelch the twinge of resentment that hit her at knowing he had inherited Jordan's position. It wasn't his fault, she reminded herself.

"I'm preparing to start a new job myself," she said, tamping down on her emotions. "I thought it would be helpful to supplement the textbooks with some visual aids, or whatever you have available. I want the students to grasp the importance of financial management in their futures."

He poised a pen for writing. "That's commendable. Your number?"

She quoted it for him. "Did you know your predecessor?"

His face went solemn. "No, I didn't. I understand he was a fine man who was the victim of a terrible crime. I hope I can handle the job as well as I'm told he did."

She stood. "I'm sure you will. Thank you for being so helpful. I plan to open an account here, but I need to wait until school, and the paychecks, start."

He smiled and stood. "I understand."

When she left the bank, Jan drove across town to Baldwin's Steak House and entered. The place was busy. It took several minutes for the line of customers to file through, order, and pay. Once she had been escorted to a table, Jan took her plate to the buffet and made herself a generous salad. As she returned to her table, an older man who resembled Colonel Sanders of Kentucky Fried Chicken strode into the room from the back and made a beeline toward her. Lyle Baldwin owned the restaurant.

"Hi, Jan," he greeted her politely, eyeing her plate. "Let's move to a quieter spot."

When he picked up her table service and tea glass, she offered no objection and followed him to a secluded table in the far corner of the dining area. When they were seated across the table from one another, he looked up at the waitress who approached. "Bring me a cup of coffee, Harriet. And make me a small salad, please." Beneath his somewhat bossy and brusque manner was a man Jan remembered as caring and fair minded.

Harriet nodded and left.

Lyle focused on Jan, his face etched with grief. "Thank you for what you're doing. Debra and I appreciate it. Have you gotten comfortable in the house yet?"

She nodded. He referred to a small house on

Ramble Street that he and Debra owned.

"I wish you would stay with us, but I agree that this is better under the circumstances. I also understand that you need your own space. Have you formed any impressions yet?"

"Not really. I visited the park and formed a visual of the crime. I also got a lesson in law enforcement." Striving to lighten the atmosphere, she told him about the DWI episode.

He produced a wan smile. "Boomer is well known around town."

"After I left the park, I went to the bank on a phony pretext and had a look around." She didn't say which bank. It wasn't necessary.

All traces of forced levity disappeared from Lyle's face. "Something is going on there. I don't know what, or how Jordy got involved. But money has to be at the root of it. Your dad—how I miss that guy—talked about you over the years, and after his death I kept track of you from a distance. I knew when you started college and when you got your CPA license. You're the financial expert—and unknown identity—I need to dig out the information that'll tell us who killed Jordy and why."

She started to respond, but he raised a hand for silence. "Eat. Then you can tell me what you want to do first."

While she ate, he nursed his coffee and nibbled at his salad. When she finished and washed down her last bites with the remainder of her iced tea, he shoved his cup and salad bowl aside.

"I'm ready to get to work any time," she said quietly. "Why don't we start at the north side of town and work our way south? What time should I meet you, and where?" Lyle had other business investments and out of town interests, but this restaurant and the half dozen gas station-convenience stores he owned locally were the cash intensive ones with a large number of employees, so they were the focus. They had to start somewhere.

"I'll pick you up. That way your vehicle won't be parked on the lots for lengthy times and advertise your presence. Together we'll catch the scumbag who killed my boy."

Chapter 2

Kyler turned in at an almost deserted Gas & Goods, one of the gas station and convenience stores owned by Lyle Baldwin. Beneath a sky glittering with stars, the gas pumps sat below a brightly lit canopy. In the huge glass window of the main building was a neon OPEN sign.

He flexed his tight back and shoulder muscles and exited his pickup. When he lifted the nozzle from the pump, a whiff of gas joined that of fresh, clean smelling spring air. When he had filled his tank, he replaced the nozzle and went inside to pay.

Monty Griffin, a familiar character around town, was at the counter, a candy bar on it before him. He pulled a roll of coins—probably filled with some of the quarters he collected—and started to open the end of the paper wrapper. But the roll slipped from his hand, landed on the floor, and split open on the concrete floor.

Kyler immediately stooped to help the man gather his runaway coins. "Is that all of them?" he asked when he got to his feet, extending a fistful of quarters to Monty. He did another visual inspection of the floor while Monty counted.

"Yep. They're all here," the elderly beanpole declared when he finished. "Thanks for the help." He paid for his candy, darted out the door, and took off up the street at a high-stepping fast pace.

"He must log twenty miles a day," the clerk said as Kyler stepped forward and handed her his credit card.

"At least," he agreed. "I suspect you log several just scampering around here." He indicated the interior of the place with a rotation of his head.

She nodded and returned his card. "You're right. And I'm sure you do even more when you're patrolling. Is there anything else I can do for you?"

He glanced back at the soda fountain. "I think something cold sounds good."

"Help yourself."

He went to the back, filled a cup with ice and Coke from a dispenser, and pushed a plastic lid onto it. When he turned and started back to the cash register, he noticed a car pulling into the reserved parking slot at the end of the building. Then he recognized Lyle Baldwin, the owner of the place, behind the wheel.

A flash of sympathy darted through him. Some people resented the man because he had so many businesses and so much money. But Lyle Baldwin had been dealt a blow that no parent should have to endure, when his son had been killed.

Kyler meant to do everything in his power to see that a killer didn't get away with the dastardly crime.

He pulled money from his pocket and paid for his soda. "How late do you have to work tonight?"

"Another three hours," Crystal said with a grimace.

"Enjoy yourself," he said as he went out the door. He got in his truck, placed his Coke in the drink caddie, and started the motor. As he rolled forward, he noticed that Mr. Baldwin had exited his car and was heading into the private entrance of the building, a woman at his side.

Then the man's companion turned enough that the bright lights lit her face. The sight made Kyler lift his foot from the gas pedal and stare over at them as he stopped to turn onto the street. It was the girl he had met in the park.

Did Mr. Baldwin have something going on with this much younger gal? The possibility made disgust curl in his midsection.

The gal, on the other hand, said she had just moved here. So how had she hooked up with one of the richest men in the area so quickly?

What was her interest in the murder?

What were her motives?

~

Jan surveyed the small but tidy office into which Mr. Baldwin led her. His wife was seated at the desk.

Debra rose and rounded the desk. "Thank you for coming," she said, embracing Jan. She stepped back and studied her more closely. "You've become the lovely young woman I foresaw in you, and I understand that you're quite accomplished. We don't know who we can trust locally, so you're a godsend to us."

Jan swallowed against a clog of emotion. "I feel like I'm jumping into a fishing expedition with no bait, but I'll do all I can to help you uncover any financial shenanigans that might be buried in your accounts. Where should I begin?"

"Right there." Debra pointed at the desk. "I have everything I could think of that you might need laid out for you. If there's anything I've forgotten, just whistle. If you have questions, at least one of us will be in the shop or out front."

Once she was alone, Jan set to work. She began by cross-referencing each part of the accounting system, reviewing the general journal, general ledger, and individual accounts—and verifying business' gross income, expenses, and costs. The only sounds in the room were the soft clack of the computer keyboard, the ticking of the clock, and the crackle of papers as she worked.

After comparing the internal and external records, and recent tax receipts to records of taxes paid and tax liabilities, she compiled a list of questions to ask the Baldwins.

Jan shoved the chair back from the desk that was now cluttered with her notes and lists and glanced up at the clock. It was after midnight.

The door opened, and the Baldwins appeared, Debra in the lead. She carried a large soda cup and a small pizza container. "The store is closed, and Crystal has gone home," she announced. "I thought you might be ready for some sustenance."

Jan's stomach growled. "This is great timing. Can I eat and talk at the same time without being rude?" She started to rise.

"Oh, no, you keep the chair," Debra ordered. "We'll sit here and answer any questions you might ahve." She placed the cup and box on the desk and went to sit beside Lyle on the small sofa positioned against the north wall. They both looked tired, but Jan knew they meant to see this through, no matter how long it took.

She chewed, swallowed a huge bite of pizza, and washed it down with soda. Then she leaned forward and clasped her hands before her on the desk. "What I've done so far is preliminary, but I'd like to ask some questions. Who takes your cash to the bank, and into what accounts is it deposited?"

"Our managers do that," Lyle said. "At this location that would be Grant Mason."

"What measures do you take to insure that all cash is reported, and to make sure employees don't steal from you? When are financial tasks usually performed, and what percentage of your sales is attributed to cash compared to credit or check payments?"

His eyes narrowed. "Are you suggesting anything in particular?"

She shook her head. "No, I'm just trying to form a clearer picture of your business operation. At this point I don't see anything out of the ordinary, but even if I did, I would prefer to wait until I've examined all the businesses before drawing any final conclusions. I would want to be positive of my findings, and their consistency, before writing a formal report."

His head moved up and down in understanding.

For another half an hour they discussed the Baldwin financial affairs, giving Jan a clear enough understanding of their empire that she could explore for possible irregularities more thoroughly. She had gotten a good start, but it looked like it would take a couple more nights to finish at this location.

She drew a huge breath and tilted her head back to study the clock on the wall—and silently prayed for strength. "I know it's hard, but we need to discuss Jordy." They had been close friends as children, but she knew very little of his growing up and adult years.

"What do you want to know?" Debra asked in a strained voice, her mouth quivering.

"I need to understand his personal life. Who were his main associates? Especially ones involved in business ventures and financial dealings."

Lyle rubbed a hand over his jaw and shot to his feet. He paced the length of the room and back, and then whirled to face her, obviously struggling for composure. "Jordan was a good boy, and then a good man. He attended Arkansas University and took a degree in accounting. Then he earned a Masters in Business Administration and came home to work for the bank."

Debra rose and went to him. She drew him back to the sofa to sit beside her and held his hand. "Two years later he married the daughter of some dear friends. Her name is Gidget, and she teaches home economics at the high school."

"Which is why we thought the school was the perfect cover for you," Lyle broke in. "The superintendent is a trusted friend, and he's agreed to confirm our cover story that you'll be teaching business classes there—should you need it for any reason."

"Jordy and Gidget had a baby boy," Debra continued. "His name is Eric, and he's almost two now. Jordy was a member of the Chamber of Commerce and several other civic organizations. He had no enemies that we know of, and he was respected in the community. It makes no sense that someone would shoot him."

Jan swallowed hard, blinking back tears. "This is too hard, so I think we should call it a night and try to get some rest. We can continue tomorrow night." She looked at Lyle for confirmation.

He nodded. "Debra has her own car and will go straight home while I circle around and drop you at the house. I'll pick you up at the same time tomorrow night and bring you back here. When you finish, we'll start on the next business. We'll keep looking until we find something."

Jan embraced each of them in turn, her heart breaking for them—all of them.

That week and the next one passed in a blur. By working increasingly longer hours, Jan completed auditing four of the six Gas & Goods businesses, leaving only two more and the steak house to do. She was beginning to doubt they would solve Jordan's murder. The park bench where he died became her refuge when she was troubled and seeking God's comfort.

She kept in almost daily touch with Terri, her assistant back in Evansville, by phone or text. If Terri needed advice, she phoned or texted.

~

As Kyler made his way across the park late Thursday afternoon, he spotted Jan Blevins at the park bench again. His gut tightened. He had been uneasy about her the first time they met after Boomer's most recent incident, but since seeing her with Lyle Baldwin he was downright distrustful. She was feeding the squirrels, so he strolled on past, hoping to be unnoticed.

"Have you had any more wheelie mishaps?"

So much for being unnoticed.

He backed up a couple of steps and sat beside her on the bench. "No, Boomer's on a time out. The judge prohibited him from being on the streets for ten days."

She snickered.

"Are you getting acquainted with our park and city?" He breathed in the scent of her subtle perfume, unsettled that he found her so pretty. A rare energy seemed to charge the air around them. Why she attracted him so strongly eluded him.

"I've driven around a bit."

"But you're back here. Is there something about this bench that's special? Or is it a meeting place?"

"I'm not meeting anyone," she said, her eyes flicking sideways. "It's beautiful here."

"You should see it in the early spring, when the

redbuds color the mountains in pink, and green foliage is popping out everywhere. Even the sky seems bluer then."

"Where are you headed?" she asked, changing the subject without answering his question.

"To the visitor center. It and the museum of the bathing industry are located in the Fordyce."

"Are the other seven bathhouses still in operation?"

"Only the Buckstaff and Quapaw still operate as bathhouses. The Ozark houses a cultural center and art gallery. The Superior is a brewery and distillery. The Lamar houses an emporium. The Maurice, the only one with a pool, closed in 1974. The oldest, the Hale, closed in 1978. And that's enough of a guided tour speech."

Her million watt smile made his heart rate kick up a notch. "Thank you for the spiel."

He pushed to his feet. "I need to get going. What about you?"

She glanced at her watch. "I was just thinking about where to eat. Do you have a recommendation?"

His good sense flew out the window—or rather into outer space. "I'm off duty in a half hour. If you'll stick around that long, I'll take you to a nice restaurant." He knew exactly where he would take her—and watch to see if she reacted.

Her eyes rounded in surprise. "I wouldn't want to put you to any trouble."

He shrugged. "It's no trouble. I have no plans for the evening."

She considered for a moment. "Okay."

Chapter 3

Jan had shocked herself when she agreed to go to supper with Ranger Winston. But when he pulled in and parked at the Baldwin Steak House, that shock skyrocketed. Every muscle in her body went tense as a guitar string. She knew from late night discussions with the Baldwins that Lyle ate here often, usually in a private room at the back. She hoped he was not present right now.

They went inside and passed a buffet loaded with steaming meats and vegetables and chilled salad makings. Kyler grinned over at her. "I hope you're hungry."

"I am."

They filled their plates from the food bar and settled at a table.

"Do you eat here a lot?' she asked after the waitress delivered their drinks and left.

"I eat here or elsewhere once or twice a week, but I

cook for myself the rest of the time."

He struck her as the self-reliant type who would do that. She figured he would be good at it—or most anything he set his mind to do.

"What about you? Do you cook or eat out regularly?"

"I'm like you. I like to eat out, but it gets old if I do it too much."

His dark eyes swept over her in detail. "You must cook some healthy meals, judging by the looks of you."

"I feel good, too. And right now I feel like eating."

The corners of his mouth hiked up, but he made no rejoinder. They focused on their plates, eating and commenting occasionally about the food. They had just returned from a trip to the dessert bar when Jan spotted Lyle Baldwin entering the buffet area from his private quarters. She quickly pulled her line of vision back to the table and grabbed her tea glass.

Kyler scrutinized her in silence, making her wonder if he had brought her here deliberately, if he had any idea of her relationship with the Baldwins. Could he have seen her with Lyle?

She breathed easier when he dug into his dessert. After a couple of bites, she leaned back in her chair, still uneasy, but threatening to explode from her need to know more about him.

"Did you grow up here?"

Kyler placed his fork beside his plate and took a healthy swig of tea. "I did. My mother died when I was ten. My dad remarried a year later. By the time I was a freshman in high school, I was living with my sister or friends. By the time I was a senior I had a part-time job and was living in my own house."

She leaned forward. "I bet that made you popular."

He nodded. "It did, but for all the wrong reasons. I was the perpetual party host and was running with a wild crowd. Fortunately, I had a sister who prayed for me and shared her concerns with her pastor. They talked me into enrolling in college. During that time away from here, their prayers were answered. I met a friend who dragged me to church with him. I came to know God rather than just knowing about Him. It put me on a new track. What about you?"

Jan blinked, taken off guard at the sudden switch of focus onto her. How much could she tell him? "When I was nine my parents divorced," she began carefully. "My mother took me and my brother with her to Indiana to live near her parents. I didn't see much of my dad after that, and I lost touch with my childhood friends."

"Did your mother remarry?"

She nodded, relieved that he had not asked where those first nine years had been lived. "After that I only saw my dad when he came to visit me and Brodie. Brodie still lives in Indiana, and he and his wife have two sons. I miss them."

"My sister is the biggest reason I came back here to work," he said. "But I always loved the park and felt it was a sign from God when they had an opening shortly after I graduated and was looking for a job."

It sounded to Jan like he had the best of situations— a job he loved, and his sister nearby. "How is your murder case progressing?"

His jaw tightened. "The investigation is ongoing."

"And you can't say any more. Okay, I get it. But I'm going to ask one more question anyhow. Do you have full confidence in all officers who were on the scene and are involved in the ongoing investigation?"

She wasn't sure why she had asked that particular question. She had just been fishing—testing his limits. But he hesitated rather than instantly telling her to shut up.

~

Kyler realized he had revealed his doubts when he didn't answer immediately. "Why would you ask that?" he probed, deciding to call her bluff. "What's your interest?"

Now she hesitated. Then she raised her chin. "I'm as curious as the next person. If I read about a murder, and then meet someone who's involved in the investigation, I'm bound to ask questions."

"You are interested, very interested," he said with satisfaction. "I want to know why."

She raked her teeth over her lower lip, the intensity of her eyes giving him the feeling she was stalling for time, concocting a way to evade his questions. "I understand that the victim had a wife and child, and that the wife teaches at the school," she said after several moments. "That means I'll be working with her. I can't help but wonder about her. Do you know her?"

He studied Jan, still suspicious of her motives, but conceding that she had a point. How had she known about the wife? Oh, yes, the newspaper story had included that information. "I went to school with her. She's a strong person, but she's having a hard time dealing with her husband's death."

Jan nodded. "Losing him that way had to be a shock. I assume the marriage was good."

He heard the question in the statement, and didn't see how it could hurt to answer it. "Everything seems to indicate it was. They both had steady jobs, got along well with their colleagues, and were active in the community. Do you fancy yourself an amateur detective?"

The impromptu question seemed to startle her, as he had intended. He tried to read her thoughts, but couldn't. If he had a lick of sense he would tell her to get lost, forget about her.

So why didn't he?

Because he wanted answers.

She didn't flinch. "No, I'm just a working girl with an extraordinary sense of curiosity. And I've been told by a couple of people that they like to bounce ideas off me. So you don't think there was money involved, like a hefty life insurance policy?"

Gutsy. He kind of liked that. She was toying with him. But he couldn't let her get to him. "Gidget has a rich father-in-law, but she didn't marry for money. A number of people have said that Mr. Baldwin expected his kids to prove themselves, earn their own way. Sure, they'll inherit big someday," he continued before she could ask—her mental wheels obviously spinning. "But both parents are in excellent health." As she surely knew, but wasn't admitting.

Her brow crinkling, she tilted her head. "Maybe you can take care of her."

*

Jan watched shock form in his expression, and realized how that must have sounded. She spread upraised palms before her. "I didn't mean anything wrong. I just thought since you indicated you have a relationship with God that you could see that she receives some kind of comfort through counseling."

He nodded. "I think I understand. Our pastor does grief counseling. The next contact I have with her, maybe I'll try to persuade her to talk to him. I'm not sure, but I'm afraid her husband's family is more involved in business and civic activities than church. Of course, I'm sure Mr. and Mrs. Baldwin are grief stricken and dealing with a certain amount of guilt. Parents tend to feel responsible for their kids no matter the circumstances."

Jan knew the Baldwins were feeling all of that. It touched her that this ranger investigator understood. She found herself wanting to tell him about her childhood neighbors, but she couldn't. Lyle and Debra wanted her presence as their outside accountant kept secret. She had to honor their wishes.

"The victim's father may feel that he was too hard on his son," she said, knowing from those late night conversations after work sessions exactly how bad Lyle felt.

"The Baldwins are much wealthier than the Abernathy family, but they seemed pleased with their son's choice of a wife."

A light bulb flared in Jan's brain. It took all her self-control to keep from revealing her reaction. She had seen that name on an account somewhere. She wanted to ask Kyler if the victim's wife had a brother by the name of Spencer Abernathy. She clamped her mouth shut and kept her face carefully blank. She would do some checking, find out more, when she met the Baldwins tonight for her next work assignment.

Forcing her brain back into focus, she bolted to her feet. "I need some ice cream to go with this cobbler."

When she returned to the table, Jan set her dish of ice cream on it. But she gave it a little unintended momentum, and it slid across the table—and off into Kyler's lap. She gasped, a hand going over her mouth. "Oh, I'm so sorry."

He grabbed the dish and set it back on the table. Then he bounced to his feet, snatched a napkin, and swiped at his pants leg. He looked up, the corners of his mouth twitching. "Are you saying you didn't want ice cream after all?"

Jan closed her eyes and sank into her chair, flushing with embarrassment. "I can't believe I did that."

He shrugged. "I made a good catch and scooped it right back into the dish. Only a little got on me."

A waitress approached, a wet cloth in her hand. "Here, Sir. I saw what happened."

"Thanks, Ma'am." He took the cloth and cleaned the remaining smear from his slacks.

"I think I'm ready to go," Jan said, not sure whether to laugh, cry, or ...what?

He chuckled. "Yeah, let's go."

Chapter 4

Once they were inside the car, Kyler turned to face Jan, all pretense of levity gone from his expression and manner. He folded his arms and leaned back slightly, wishing she would turn enough that he could see her eyes better.

His feelings about her were tumultuous. She seemed harmless, an innocent and honest sort. But he sensed there was more to her repeated presence in the park than she was admitting. She was more intense than he would expect from a young woman moving to a new location and embarking on a new career venture. And her acquaintance with Mr. Baldwin, whom she had avoided speaking to this evening, indicated there was another side to her. He wanted her to be as innocent as she appeared. But he sensed she had come to Hot Springs for a deeper reason.

Why? He wished she would get honest about it.

On the other hand, she had said that others liked to bounce ideas off her. What would it hurt to test her?

"Would you care to toss some thoughts around with me?"

She met his gaze without flinching. "Sure. I'll be a wall. Throw some jello at me and see if anything sticks. What's chasing around in your head that needs organizing?"

"I can't talk about what the police are doing or saying, but I don't see anything wrong with two friends sharing thoughts and concerns regarding a murder. How much do you remember from the newspaper stories about the victim?"

Her face crinkled in thought. "He worked for a bank, so he undoubtedly spent a great deal of time with his co-workers. But he would also have interacted with a lot of bank customers—in case you're wondering who his closest associates were."

He suppressed a grin. "You're on track. I knew him casually, but not in a personal way like I did his wife's family."

"What about friends they would have had as a couple?"

"Well, his wife worked, too. I've heard Gidget mention having colleagues over for get-togethers." He thought about that. "In fact, now that I think about it, she used to talk about one couple in particular. I can't remember a name, but the wife taught in the junior high, and I believe the husband did as well. No, wait. He didn't teach. He was the junior high principal."

"They must have been pretty good friends for you

to remember that much. Could there have been any conflict there?" She raised a palm. "I know I'm reaching here, but you never know when jello might stick."

He nodded, something niggling at his brain.

She studied him, as if reading his mind. "What is it?"

Suddenly he remembered. "I never heard of any conflict, but I recall my sister mentioning that her daughter's principal resigned suddenly and left in December. Her daughter's in junior high."

"That had to be the friends," she said, genuine interest lacing her tone. "Did you hear any reason for an administrator leaving in mid-year?"

He searched his memory. "It seems she said something about him having elderly parents who were ailing, and the couple moved to be near them."

Even as he said the words, unease crept over him. Had something been missed?

Jan voiced his thoughts. "Could there be more to his disappearance than meets the eye?"

"I don't know," he said thoughtfully.

She tilted her head in a way that made him think he could hear the wheels turning in it. "Do you think there's a connection? The timing seems strangely coincidental, as if something was going on in the background. I think you should find out where that couple went."

He grinned. "You're thinking like an investigator. And I think you're right. I'll talk to my sister again, and then check some other sources if she can't tell me anything about them."

A phone interrupted what he started to say next. It wasn't his ring tone.

She pulled hers from her purse and checked the ID. "Hello," she said pleasantly, and then listened for a bit.

"Seven o'clock will be fine," she said and disconnected.

Apparently, she had just made a date. The idea grated at him. Bouncing thoughts off her no longer held any appeal. He faced forward and started the motor. "It sounds like you need to go. Since I picked you up at the park, I assume you have a vehicle parked nearby."

"Yes, you can let me out there."

He drove to the park in silence, but questions created a racket in his brain. Who had she arranged to meet?

When he pulled to the curb where he had picked her up, she pushed the door open and hopped out. "Thank you for the meal," she said, leaning inside the opening. Then she shut the door and walked away.

Kyler sat and watched her hike to a silver Camaro and get inside. Then, questioning his sanity, he eased into traffic at a distance behind her. She drove to a small house on a residential street and went inside.

Without understanding the depth of his nosiness, Kyler parked around a corner and continued to watch the house. Minutes later, at seven o'clock, a car drove up the street and parked. When he recognized Mr. Baldwin at the wheel, his hands clenched on the steering wheel.

Jan emerged from the building and got into the

man's car.

Kyler watched the car roll up the street. Then he started his own vehicle and followed them at a discreet distance.

~

Lyle drove up to Gas & Goods #5 and ushered Jan in through the private entrance to where his wife waited. After greetings, the couple left Jan alone to work undisturbed.

Before beginning her usual review, Jan searched the company employee records. She found a Spencer Abernathy listed, and it looked like he worked at this particular location. For some reason that fact made her uneasy.

The door opened, and a head peeked inside. It was the guy she had seen out front when she and Lyle arrived. Could he be Abernathy?

"Hello, Ma'am. Can I bring you anything, a cold soda or a snack?" The odor of fresh gasoline drifted from him. A mop of reddish brown hair tumbled to his shoulders. His over friendly manner struck her as bordering on nosiness, and put her on edge.

"No, thank you," she said politely. "I had a big supper, and I'm still full."

He pulled back a bit, but didn't close the door. "I'm the manager. If I can be of any help to you, don't hesitate to ask." His gaze flicked over the desk and the items spread across it.

Jan got the uneasy feeling he wanted to ask what she was doing. She peered at his employee name tag. It wasn't clear enough to read from that distance, but it was too short to be Abernathy. "Tell Uncle Lyle I'm downloading that program he wants."

There, that would probably confuse Lyle, but it should alert him that she was being visited, and maybe put this guy in a spot. If he was being nosy, and had slipped around behind the boss's back to peek in on her, he now had to say something and alert Lyle that he had spoken to her—or say nothing and risk Jan mentioning whether her message had been relayed.

He disappeared, and Jan returned to work. She began as usual, reviewing ledger and journal entries and account balances. Everything was routine for a half hour or so. But when she compared the store's financial statements to the bank balance, she received a surprise. Thinking she has missed something, or made an error, she went back over everything in more detail.

Jan had been on the alert for money shortages. But what she had here was *too much* money. She was checking deposits shown on bank statements to office records when the Baldwin couple returned earlier than usual, Mrs. Baldwin bearing her usual offerings of a snack and soda.

Jan flexed her tight shoulder muscles and massaged the nape of her neck. Then she smiled and reached for the frosty soda.

"Uncle Lyle? And what program?" Lyle Baldwin's brow-raised scrutiny was calm but intense, his tone rife with question.

Jan swigged thirstily and set the soda down. "An employee opened the door and asked if I needed anything. In case he was snooping, I gave him a message for you."

Lyle frowned. "That's what I surmised. Does that look on your face mean you're just tired, or is there a problem?"

"Both." She motioned for the couple to be seated, and waited until they were settled before saying more. She leaned forward on her elbows on the desk. "I've found a discrepancy. You have too much money."

Both faces went wide-eyed with surprise.

"That's certainly not something I expected to hear," Lyle said, his posture becoming more relaxed.

"I was trying to figure out why your balance is higher than it should be. This audit may take a little longer than the earlier ones."

"Do you want to go home and get some rest, and then continue tomorrow night?"

She shook her head. "I'd rather work a little later, if you don't mind waiting for me."

"This is why you're here," Lyle assured her. "And the sooner we identify any problems, the better I like it."

"Who makes the deposits?" she asked, knowing she was repeating an earlier question, but needing to be certain.

"The managers."

She frowned. "Is that plural, as in for your businesses overall, or for each one individually?"

"Each one," he said. "Jeb Adams, the manager you met, is the night manager here. Spencer Abernathy is the day manager. They both make deposits."

"I assume you trust both of them implicitly."

Mr. and Mrs. Baldwin exchanged glances, concern etching their features.

"Spencer is Jordan's brother-in-law," Debra said, clearly troubled. "I can't believe he would do anything wrong. And I don't understand how there can be too much money in the account, or how anything could be wrong if there is."

"I'm not saying anything is wrong." Jan took another drink from her soda and plucked a cashew from the container Debra had placed on the desk.

Lyle stood. "Let's make ourselves scarce and give her the time she needs to work."

As they left the room, Jan turned back to the computer. During their conversation, an idea had begun to form in her mind. She dug deeper, tracing backward through the accounts.

~

Kyler sat in his car, parked in the small lot across the street from Baldwin's Gas & Goods #5. He wasn't sure why he was hanging around, conducting a personal surveillance like this. There was something about Jan that drove him to the stupidity of following her around and spying on a man's business.

It appeared that something was going on between the young woman and older man. But something—maybe just a sense of hope—had him sneaking around trying to find out exactly what kind of relationship they had.

The place had been booming with business during the hour or more he had been sitting here. The subjects were still inside. Nothing was happening here except the wasting of his time.

As that thought crossed his mind, a car caught his attention. As it pulled up to a pump, he recognized the driver. It was Curtis Sidebottom, who worked as an attendant at the Buckstaff Bathhouse.

While Curtis was pumping gas into his truck, the manager emerged from the convenience store and approached the older vehicle. He took a wet cloth from a bucket, wiped the windshield, then grabbed the end of the towel that dangled from his hip pocket and dried the glass. When finished, he walked around to the rear of the vehicle.

Curtis replaced the pump nozzle and twisted the cap onto his gas tank. Then he walked back to join the manager. He made a furtive glance around, and then popped the trunk lid. He raised it and pulled out a gym bag.

The manager took it and headed back to the store. Curtis slammed the trunk lid closed and followed him.

Curious, and alarmed, Kyler forced himself to sit motionless. He wanted to run over there and get a look inside that bag. But he couldn't. He had no grounds for such an action.

What he did have was a barrel of suspicions. He knew that gambling took place outside the confines of Oaklawn Park, one of the biggest tourist attractions in Arkansas and one of the best attended thoroughbred race tracks in America. Could these two be mixed up in something like that?

Through the glass window he could see Curtis paying for his gas at the counter. Then the guy came back outside, climbed in his car, and drove away. But Kyler still sat there, obstinately reluctant to go home—as he should.

At midnight the place closed, and the employees left. But two cars remained near the side entrance. Finally, about one a.m., a woman emerged, got in one car, and drove away. A couple of minutes later Jan stepped through the doorway and went to the other car. Mr. Baldwin emerged, locked the entrance door, and got behind the wheel.

Mentally berating himself, Kyler watched the car head up the street, started his truck, and once again followed at a distance. As expected, Mr. Baldwin drove to Jan's house and parked. But he did not get out. He simply sat there and watched while Jan got out and went inside.

Chapter 5

As Jan drove down Central Avenue Friday morning, her gaze gravitated automatically to the park, searching for the sight of a ranger uniform. She was oddly disappointed at not seeing Kyler, and wondered what he would think if he knew her real identity and purpose. She quickly pushed aside such thoughts. Facing forward, she replaced thoughts of him with reviewing ways money launderers operated.

They sometimes placed dirty money in legitimate businesses to clean it. Some used cash-intense businesses like bars, car washes, check-cashing stores, or convenience stores as fronts. The launderer combined the dirty money with the company's clean revenues—reporting higher revenues from the legitimate business than it was really earning. Or they simply hid the dirty money in the company's legitimate bank accounts in hopes that authorities would not compare the bank balance to the financial statements.

It didn't really make sense in this case. Lyle was searching for answers, not hiding them.

Could either of those managers at the Gas & Goods #5 be brash enough to use their employer's company to launder money? And, if so, why did they need to launder money? Money laundering, in its simplest form, was disguising the origin of money obtained through illegal activities so it appeared to be obtained from legal sources, and law enforcement officials couldn't seize it.

With all that in mind, Jan had dug deeper the past two evenings, tracing backward through the accounts. And the deeper she dug, the more convinced she became that something like that was happening here. It was easy enough to locate the extra deposits. Now she had to figure out where the money was coming from, who was depositing it, and in what kind of racket they were involved.

The most common criminals she could think of who needed to launder money were drug traffickers, embezzlers, corrupt politicians and public officials, mobsters, terrorists, and con artists. The managers were the logical suspects. They handled those deposits. Could Jordan's young brother-in-law be involved in white collar crime? Jan hoped not. The night manager peeking in on her made her see him as a more likely culprit.

She was asking herself how any of this could be related to Jordan's murder when another thought—a horrible one—occurred to her. Could he have been using his father's business to funnel money? As a banker, he would certainly know how such things worked.

Jan pulled in at the bank and parked in the lot, still not entirely certain how to advise Lyle and Debra. Lyle didn't want anyone to know her identity, so she couldn't present herself to the bank officers as an auditor and ask questions about the Baldwin accounts. He also didn't want to approach any bank or law enforcement people until she had finished examining the records at all of his businesses.

Jan knew that bank employees received some anti-money laundering training and were instructed to report any suspicious activity. But identifying suspicious activity was not always easy. Her gut said answers were here in this building, but she didn't know how to get at them. All she could do at this point was observe the facility and get to know more of the personnel.

Not sure why she was here, but needing to do something, talk to someone or see something, Jan entered the bank and approached the front desk. "I'd like to speak to Mr. Nichols again," she said, thinking she could ask about the materials she had requested.

The woman frowned. "He's not in right now. Can someone else help you?"

Jan hated subterfuge, but she had no better ideas. "Do you have someone who would be willing to represent banking for Career Day at the high school?"

A man who was walking across the lobby stopped, his eyes flicking over her in assessment. "I'm Mike

Crenshaw, the Operations Manager. May I help you with something?" His smile was bright, his dark suit impeccable and expensive. Slightly below medium height, with razor cut dark hair, he exuded confidence and friendliness that bordered on phony.

"I'm Jan Blevins, and I'm new in town," she explained quickly. "I spoke to Mr. Nichols earlier regarding obtaining materials from you about the banking industry to supplement the textbooks I'll be using in my business classes."

His smile widened. "Why don't we step into my office and discuss your needs? I assume it'll only take a few minutes."

He escorted her to one of the nearest offices, motioned her to a chair, and went behind the desk. "Am I to understand that you'll be teaching in our school district?"

She nodded. "Your district superintendent gave me a contract to teach at the high school." He had, so she could honestly make such a statement if needed. It was blank.

"Welcome to our town," he said, leaning forward. "Now, what exactly is it you need from us?"

She thought fast, recalling her own school experiences. "I need one or two bank officers to spend a couple of hours at our high school Career Day. We'd like for you to give the students a presentation about jobs in banking, the kind of education required, and some insights into the kinds of special training and guidelines to expect once they're employed by a bank—like confidentiality agreements, bank and online security, watching for suspicious accounts, and anti-laundering training."

His brows rose. "You seem quite knowledgeable. That's commendable. I'll bring up the matter at a board meeting and see if there are any volunteers."

"Thank you." She stood, her gut in knots.

~

Kyler hiked across the park grounds, making rounds. He automatically looped around past the park bench where Jordan Baldwin had died, and Miss Blevins liked to sit.

The woman puzzled him, and that made him nervous. He didn't like it. But he couldn't stop her image from popping into his mind, or his thoughts from drifting to her.

He shook his head, as if to rid it of those thoughts, and headed toward the Buckstaff. A huge structure, the exterior consisted of cream colored brick and stucco finishes, spandrels, friezes, cornices and a parapet in a Neo classical Revival style. The entrance had seven bays divided by engaged columns with pavilions flanking the north and south ends.

Inside, a flow of tourists moved about. He looked around, hoping to spot Curtis. When he didn't see the young man, he approached the front desk where Henry, the manager, stood talking to an older couple. When the two continued up the hallway, Henry faced Kyler.

"How are things?" White teeth sparkled in a ruddy face.

"It's a beautiful day—and peaceful. What more

could I ask?"

"You just making rounds, or do you need something?"

"I'm on rounds, but I notice that Curtis isn't here."

"He's off today."

"You reckon maybe he's playing the ponies?"

Henry grimaced. "It's very likely."

Kyler detected concern in the manager's expression. "What is it?"

The man hesitated. "I don't want to stir up anything, but one day last week he showed up for work with a freshly busted lip. I asked him about it, and he made a joke about his own clumsiness. I never did find out what happened."

"Do you think he's in trouble over gambling problems?"

Henry shook his head and shrugged. "I don't know. I hope not."

Kyler moved on, more uneasy than ever about the young bathhouse attendant. When he finished his shift, he stopped by the police station.

"He's on our radar," the sheriff said when Kyler asked about Curtis and told him about the split lip. Built like a football player and tough as nails, Ben Proctor was a buddy as well as a law enforcement officer associate.

"Does he have a gambling problem?"

Ben's head moved up and down. "I'm afraid so."

"Is he in deep enough to have been lured into something bad? I saw him hand the manager a bag while gassing up his car at one of Baldwin's Gas &

Goods places."

Ben rubbed his jaw. "We're not sure. There may be a new gambling ring operating in the area. If there is, and he's part of it, he's in deep trouble."

"I think I'll run out to the race track and talk to some people. If that won't step on any toes," he added.

The sheriff gave him a lopsided grin. "You know the rule. You have to share if you latch onto anything useful."

Kyler snapped a half salute and walked away.

Later that evening, he arrived home and popped a frozen dinner in the microwave, too tired to cook. Then he called Ben.

"Information wasn't plentiful, but I did get a tidbit. An old acquaintance confirmed that Curtis is betting more than he can afford. And..."

He paused, unsure whether to bother mentioning the other person he had asked about.

"And what?" the sheriff prodded. "You know details that seem insignificant can prove unexpectedly important."

Kyler drew a long breath. "My sister and her husband have some friends who resigned their positions in the middle of the school term and left town. I got to thinking about it and wondering why they would do that in such a hurry."

"Are you talking about the junior high principal and his wife?"

"Yeah. It seems he was a regular at the track on weekends, and he placed bets—some heavy ones—by phone during the week."

"It sounds like he might have gotten in a little too deep and taken off, running from creditors. If that's the case, it's not good."

No, it wasn't.

Kyler didn't see any connections to the murder case, but instinct drove him to dig deeper.

~

Saturday morning, Jan decided it was time to replenish her empty fridge. When she got in her car to leave, she noticed that her gas tank was low. Since the Gas & Goods where she had worked Thursday night was on the way to the grocery store, she pulled in there and filled her tank.

When she went inside to pay, the manager, whom she now knew to be Jeb Adams, was behind the counter. When the bell over the door jangled, he looked her way. He smiled and stepped closer to the counter top. "Hello, Ma'am. Your uncle isn't here right now, in case you're looking for him."

"No, I just needed gas." She pulled out her wallet and extracted a twenty. She paid for everything in cash, rather than using her credit card that bore her correct name.

"I'll take care of her," Jeb told the clerk. The girl stepped back, her look telling Jan she wasn't accustomed to such help.

He took the bill and put it in the register. "I'm glad Spencer and I traded shifts today. Will you and the boss be visiting later tonight?" He returned her change.

"Not tonight," she said, not wanting to say any more

than necessary.

He eyed her more seriously. "Is there a problem?"

"He had a virus on his computer. I think it's clean now, but I may check it later."

"If you come again, I'll be happy to buy you a cup of coffee, or whatever you prefer."

"Maybe I'll let you," she said, turning and heading out the door, while resolving that would never happen. She got in her car and started the motor, glancing over as she pulled away from the pump. Through the glass window she saw that Jeb had his phone to his ear.

She drove to the grocery store and bought the items on her list. When she emerged, she opened the back passenger door for the carryout boy to put the bags in the seat. As he walked away, she started to get in the car and noticed a folded slip of paper under her windshield wiper.

She pulled it free and opened it.

Meet me at the thermal springs on Central at one o'clock if you want to know more about your problem.

Alarmed, Jan tucked the note in her purse and scooted behind the wheel. The smart thing to do would probably be to ignore the note, she reasoned as she drove to her house. But curiosity wouldn't let her do that.

The thermal springs were in the open, right beside the highway. The park and streets were well patrolled. She should be safe. If there was any chance of gaining information that would help identify Jordan's killer, she had to get it.

At ten minutes before one o'clock, she found a parking place around the corner half a block from the springs, and parked at the curb. She got out, scanning the area, and made her way to a bench near the rock rimmed ledge from which faucets protruded.

She sat. And sat. Checked her watch every couple of minutes. But no one came. Finally, at one-forty-five, she considered it a bust, picked up her purse, and headed back to her car.

Jan gasped when she arrived. Both tires next to the curb had been slashed. She rounded the car and found that the more visible ones next to the street were okay. She was reaching for her phone when she spied another folded piece of paper under her wiper.

She reached for it, clenching her teeth as anger boiled inside her. Her hands trembled as she unfolded it. The lettering was big and bold.

GET OUT OF THIS TOWN.

Chapter 6

Kyler glanced at the park bench. Jan wasn't there. His gaze swept the area, and stopped abruptly when he spotted her at the curb, staring at a piece of paper in her hand. Then his line of vision lowered, and he saw that her tires had been slashed. He broke into a run.

"What happened?" he asked when he reached her.

She looked up, shaking her head in bewilderment. Fear and confusion lined her face. "Someone left a note on my windshield at the gas station saying to meet them here at the springs at one o'clock. I came, but no one ever met me. I started to leave, and this is what I found."

"Just now?"

She nodded.

He reached for the paper. "Let me see that."

She nodded again and handed it to him.

He read it and fought for control. "You're in danger.

Why?" The need to protect her blocked everything else from his mind.

"I don't know." Her words were low and unsteady.

He reached for his phone and called the police station. "I have a case of vandalism, slashed tires and a threatening note, over here by Bathhouse Row. Send someone to take a report."

"You aren't expected to deal with this kind of thing, are you?" Jan asked as he disconnected.

"Of course, I am. We act as law enforcement officers in instances of vandalism or when people need protection, and cooperate with our local police department."

She seemed relieved. "You're more versatile than I realized."

A half hour later, when the police had their questions answered, the note in their possession, and were gone Kyler was able to speak to Jan. "Would you like me to call a tow truck for you?"

"Please," she said softly. "I don't know who to call for that. But I guess I need to contact my insurance company." By now she sounded less shaken than when he arrived.

"I'll give you a ride if you like."

"Thank you."

As the deputy left, the tow truck rolled down the street and stopped alongside them. A bushy headed older man poked his head out the window. "Howdy, Winston. I take it this is the vehicle I'm after."

"Yep. The tires over here next to the curb are slashed. If you'll drag the car to your place, I'll follow with this lady. It's her car."

The driver gave him a thumb salute and pulled his head back inside the truck.

By now Jan had reached her insurance agent. Having moved several steps further away for privacy, she carried on a phone discussion while Milton hooked her car to the tow truck and drove away. When she disconnected, Kyler approached and took her arm. "My department vehicle is around the block."

At Milton's garage, she approved the purchase of two new tires and paid for them with cash. Milton and his helper worked quickly and soon had her ready to roll.

"Thanks for everything," she said to Kyler, gripping the door handle.

"I wish I could have done more." His eyes met hers, wishing he could draw her into his arms. "Are you sure you're okay?"

She drew a fortifying breath. "I will be."

He glanced at his watch. "I have a guided tour scheduled in an hour, but I have time to follow you home."

She shook her head. "That's not necessary." She opened the door and got in the car.

He watched her drive away, and then forced his mind onto his next duties. But he couldn't stop thinking about her.

Why was Jan being threatened?

Why did it matter so much to him, beyond the normal scope of his job?

~

Jan tossed and tumbled, unable to sleep. A mountain of questions bombarded her. Who had vandalized her car and threatened her? Why? Who was running money through at least one of Lyle's accounts?

Why had Jordan been killed? Why hadn't God protected him? Sadness and grief weighed her spirit.

If her grief was this heavy, how could the Baldwins bear it? Would God help them want to go on living? Did He care?

Sometime after midnight Jan crawled out of bed and booted her computer. She went to an Internet search engine and typed the name of the night manager at the business with the extra money funneled into its account. She had almost given up finding anything when she spied a single article about Jeb Adams being arrested on a domestic violence charge. It seemed that he and his live-in girlfriend fought a lot. But that didn't tell her anything about his work or any financial activities in which he might be involved.

She did a search on Spencer Abernathy, and had more luck. But the articles she found were all positive—a wedding announcement photo and write-up, a couple of news items about civic organizations, with him being involved. He seemed squeaky clean.

Unable to think of anything else to research, she shut down the computer and went back to bed.

In spite of her short sleep, Jan woke early Sunday morning. She sat on the side of the bed, pondering whether to go to church. After several moments she picked up her phone and dialed.

"Would you consider going to church with me?" she asked when Debra Baldwin answered. "I feel I need to go, but I don't think I can do it alone."

Silence vibrated across the line. "Which church?"

Jan swallowed. "The one on Park Place." It was where her daddy had taken his family. And Jordan and his sister had often gone with them.

"I don't know," the woman said hesitantly. "Let me ask Lyle."

Jan could hear voices in the background, but couldn't distinguish the words. Then Debra returned. "He says, considering the way you're helping us, we can't turn down the only thing you've asked of us."

"Thank you," she breathed shallowly.

The last time she had been in this church was when she slipped into a back pew at Jordan's funeral. She had spoken briefly to the family at the end of the service, but then had left for home immediately rather than going to the cemetery and gathering for a meal afterward.

As if he knew they were there, the pastor spoke of dealing with a heartbreaking loss.

"When a loved one is taken and we are left behind, we may think the loss is more than we can bear. But when grief overwhelms us, our greatest help comes from trusting God. Our greatest comfort is in knowing He is in control. He will always be near."

As tears wet their faces, Debra drew Jan to her with one arm and Lyle with the other. The three of them wept together, and Jan sensed God's comforting presence. The words were reassuring, but their biggest solace seemed to be in just sitting together, listening in silence, and hugging and weeping together when sorrow overcame them.

~

Monday morning Kyler woke tired from loss of sleep. Still troubled, he scrounged a donut and cup of coffee and placed his laptop on the kitchen table. He gulped the donut while the computer booted, and then burned his lip swigging the hot coffee.

Hissing and blowing through his teeth, he pulled up a search engine and began a search for Jan Blevins, wanting to know more about her. But he could find nothing on anyone by that name whose picture looked anything like his Jan.

His Jan? He blinked and shook his head. She was getting to him more than he realized.

He stared at the computer screen, his thoughts tumbling. The idea was farfetched, but could she be someone other than who she professed to be? The more he thought about it, the more it nagged at him.

He dressed and went to work. When he entered the ranger station, he pulled out his phone and dialed the sheriff's private number.

"Ben, can you send a deputy over here with a fingerprint kit?"

"What's the problem?"

Kyler rubbed his jaw. "I'm not sure. I'd just like to confirm an identity. There was a vandalism incident over here Saturday, and..."

"I remember," the sheriff interrupted. "You want us

to look for prints on that lady's tires? We already did that—with no luck."

"Uh, that was a good idea, but it's not what I had in mind. I gave her a ride to the garage to pick up her car, and her prints should be in my truck."

Silence. Then Ben cleared his throat. "Are you thinking there's something ...oh, never mind. Whatever's bugging you, let's get it settled. I'll send someone to take prints, and then let you know who owns 'em."

"I need to get going, but I'll leave my truck key here in the office."

He broke the connection, replaced his hat on his head, and headed out the door. Later that morning, he couldn't believe his eyes when he spotted Jan seated on the park bench again. When he walked closer, he saw that she was crying.

A light bulb went off in his brain, bringing him to a jolting halt. Jan didn't have a thing for Lyle Baldwin. It was the son.

And Lyle approved?

That didn't ring right. Jordan Baldwin had been married. He had a child.

Kyler's jaw tightened. He slid onto the bench next to her, determined to get some answers. "You're here again. There's obviously a reason related to our murder investigation. What is it?"

She didn't look at him, but her chin quivered. "I just feel bad about what happened," she said remotely.

He reached over and turned her face toward him. "I've seen you with the man's dad. Why?"

The tension in her was readable. Her throat moved as she swallowed. Her eyes held anguish. Tears spilled from them. "I want to find out who killed him," she ground out in muffled harshness. "He deserves justice, and to have his name cleared. He was a good man." Her words had grown fierce on the last sentence.

Kyler started to ask how she knew that, but was interrupted by the pinging of his phone. He wanted to ignore it, but checked the ID. When he saw that the text was from Ben, he read it.

Prints belong to someone by the name of Janelle Evans.

Evans. His brain kicked into rapid speed, a kaleidoscope of images and thoughts flashing through it.

And then he knew. She had to be the daughter of Damien Evans, Baldwin's long time right hand man—until his death a few years ago.

He refocused on her, studying her from a new perspective. "I think I like the name Janelle better than Jan."

Her eyes rounded in shock. "You know?" The question came out in a hoarse whisper.

"Only your name. Why don't you tell me about it? Was your dad Damien Evans?"

She drew in a ragged breath and gazed upward. Then she gave her head a shake. "Yes."

"How well did you know Jordan Baldwin?"

She lowered her gaze to meet his. "He was my first boyfriend," she said shakily, a tiny smile peeking through her pain. "He gave me my first kiss and asked me to marry him."

A quick stab of something hit him in the gut. Jealousy? "What did you say?"

She emitted a choked little laugh. "I bopped him on the head and ran away. I was six, and he was seven."

His mouth twitched. "Did anything ever change?"

She shrugged. "Everything changed. Not all at once, but faster than anyone expected."

"Why don't you start at the beginning?"

Her expression took on a faraway look, as if lost in the past. "My dad worked for Jordy and Michelle's dad. We lived a couple of blocks from them, and we kids spent a lot of time playing together. Jordy and Michelle went to church with us most Sundays. Debra and Lyle attended there as well, but they weren't as regular. Lyle was building up his business back then," she explained with a spreading of her hands. "Then it all ended."

He recalled hearing stories during his teens about Baldwin and Evans buying up property. "When? How?"

"When our parents divorced, Mother wouldn't bring me and Brodie back here to see Daddy. It broke his heart. He came to see us as often as he could, even after she remarried. The only reason he didn't fight her for custody of us was because he felt that would only hurt me and Brodie more."

He thought he knew, but he asked anyhow. "How come you're back now?"

"Lyle asked me to help him find out why Jordy was murdered."

He frowned. "Are you in law enforcement?"

She grinned now, her expression clearing a little. "Hardly." She wiped her eyes with a tissue. "I'm here as their auditor. I'm a CPA, and Lyle knew that. I hadn't realized it until recently, but he kept track of me and Brodie. Last month he called and said the police weren't having any success finding his son's killer. He asked me to come and audit each of his businesses, looking for anything that could possibly be connected to Jordy's death."

That explained her late meetings with the man. Lyle picked her up and took her home so her car would not be parked on his lots all night and draw attention. "I've seen you enter a couple of his Gas & Goods businesses with him. You do your work after the heavy business hours are over and most of the employees are gone, don't you?"

She nodded. "Debra goes in and has things laid out so I can get right to work as soon as we arrive."

The wife was even present. His respect for Jan…Janelle…skyrocketed, along with admiration for her professional work.

She met his gaze directly. "Are you going to tell me to stop my involvement?"

"Would it do any good if I did?"

She shook her head. "No."

Chapter 7

"So, can we work together?"

Her question jolted Kyler. He wasn't sure it was a wise idea, but it had an abnormal appeal. The smile that crossed her face made her so pretty she stole his breath.

Instinct told him that her beauty was more than skin deep. Those dark eyes glinted even though they were protected from the ninety-degree sun by the shade of the trees, and subtle highlights reflected from her dark hair. But her integrity was no longer clouded.

A faint blush tinted Jan's ...Janelle's face, making him realize he'd been staring.

He pushed off the bench, took her hand, and tugged her up beside him. "Let's talk about it. I think better when I'm in motion."

She let him lead her across the lawn toward the thermal fountain next to Central Avenue.

"Do you work for an accounting agency?"

She looked over at him, a ghost of a smile tugging at her mouth. "I have my own CPA office."

"I'm impressed. Is it running itself while you're away?"

"My assistant is in charge. Tax season is over, so Terri can handle it. I check in with her regularly, and she contacts me when she runs into problems."

"I assume this office is in Indiana."

"Yes. From the time Mother left here with us, I always planned to come back after I finished school. But after Daddy died when I was fifteen, I dropped the idea and stayed in Evansville."

"When will you be going back there?"

She halted by the public fountain at the end of the street. "When we finish auditing all of Lyle's businesses—or find the answers."

"How are you progressing?"

"We've been working our way north to south across town, examining each business one by one. We should finish in a few more days."

She pulled her hand from his and trailed it in the steaming one-hundred-forty-three degree water. "I had forgotten how hot it is," she said, laughing as she wiped her hand on the leg of her white capris pants.

Kyler cupped his hands, filled them, and drank. He glanced around at others who were doing the same, or filling water bottles and jugs, as people were encouraged to do. Approximately seven hundred thousand gallons of thermal waters were collected each day in the Hot Springs Reservoir.

"Have you learned anything helpful to the case yet?"

She gazed across the lawn. "I'm not sure."

"Do you have time to walk the promenade?"

The fountain was at the beginning of the Grand Promenade, a half-mile of brick paved walkway behind Bathhouse Row. Running parallel with Central Avenue and the row, it looped north-south on the hillside and offered scenic views of the historic downtown, the Arlington Lawn, the hot springs cascade, and quartz veins in the sandstone and tufu cliffs.

"That sounded like you might have learned something," he said as they headed to the walkway.

"It means I've found that too much money is being deposited in the account of one of the businesses. I need to check further and find out where that money is coming from and going to."

"You suspect someone is funneling dirty money?"

"Something like that," she admitted, not breaking pace.

"Would it happen to be the location where you were Thursday night?"

She stopped mid-stride and faced him. "Why do you ask? And how do you know where I was Thursday night?"

He gulped guiltily. "I saw you."

Her eyes narrowed. "You followed me, didn't you? And saw me with Lyle."

He nodded.

"You formed opinions, didn't you?"

There would be no escaping. "I formed questions. I

already had some, which is the reason I followed you. Something about the way you came here," he said, moving a hand in an arc that encompassed the park, "told me you had more on your mind than you admitted."

She inhaled deeply and emitted the breath in a huff. "Okay, I'll concede that you had cause for suspicion. But it doesn't explain the rest of your question. It sounds like you saw or heard something."

"I saw a young man who works as an attendant at the Buckstaff handing the night manager a bag."

Her eyes raked over him. Then her expression took on an introspective look, and her head began to nod slowly in comprehension. "I think that manager is funneling dirty money through his boss's business. While I was working, the guy opened the office door to offer me a soda and snack. I think it was a pretext to peek in while I was working. He may suspect I'm onto him."

"I can understand why Lyle wanted an anonymous expert examining his books. And someone who believed in his son."

Her hands went to her hips. "Jordy was an honest man. Lyle says the police think he had to have been involved in something illegal to end up the way he did. We intend to prove we're right." She paused, scrutinizing him. "I've told you what little I know. What can you tell me? And don't say Jordan Baldwin was crooked. He wasn't." Her tone had grown fierce.

He gave her a small grin. "I'm keeping an open mind."

She glanced down at his feet. "You said you think better in motion. So move, and talk."

He chuckled. "Okay. The bath attendant's name is Curtis, and the bathhouse manager said he came to work last week with some face damage. I went out to the race track and asked around about him. The word is that he's another poor guy looking for a get-rich-quick way to supplement his meager income, and he may have ended up getting poorer and poorer by betting more than he could afford to lose."

"So you think he's an addicted gambler who has been drawn into some kind of gambling ring?"

"That's my guess."

She kept walking, glancing aside occasionally at the picturesque sight of the hot springs bubbling up from the ground. "I'm guessing that Jeb, the night manager, is running it, or is at least involved in running it. And I've made him nervous. But I don't see how it connects to Jordy's death."

A squirrel scampered across the walkway in front of them and raced up a tree. They stopped to watch it and listen to its chatter, and followed its path back down the tree. Then they resumed walking.

~

Janelle hiked faster, avoiding visual and physical contact with Kyler. The touch of his hand over hers at the beginning of their hike had sent unexpected warmth surging up her arm. She had not met his gaze since then, afraid of what she might read there.

"I didn't know your childhood friend well," he said, catching up and pacing alongside her. "But Jordan

Baldwin seemed like a nice guy. I remember seeing a picture of his wife and baby on his desk when I was at the bank on business."

She slowed down a bit. When she did, he took her arm and guided her to one of the benches positioned at intervals along the path. He sat and pulled her down beside him.

When he turned her face so their eyes met, Janelle couldn't look away. "What are you saying?"

"It looks like there's money laundering behind all this. But there are mixed opinions about whether Jordan was involved." His tone was clipped.

"He was involved, all right," she snapped in flaring indignation. "He was a victim. He found out something, and it cost him his life."

As Kyler studied her, she imagined she could hear the wheels turning in his brain.

"Janelle," he said slowly. "I want you to be right, but I have to maintain objectivity. I have nothing convincing me that your friend was anything but an honorable man. But I have to check every avenue."

His words held a ring of sincerity. Janelle drew a shaky breath. "I understand your position. I hope you understand mine."

~

Kyler nodded, sympathy for her rising in his chest. And something else. He had been inexplicably attracted to her from his first meeting with her. Now that he was seeing her in a new light, that attraction was growing. He forced his gaze from her face and stared across the landscape for several moments. Then he looked back at her, debating how much to share.

"Do you think you can be objective if we talk about how he died?"

Her gaze intensified, piercing him. Then she nodded. "I think so."

He cleared his throat and indicated the distant bench with a jerk of his head. "He was found sitting slumped there, his hat over his eyes."

"You mean it looked like he was sleeping?"

"Yes. His position makes us think it wasn't a violent confrontation. He never put up a struggle."

She frowned. "You mean it looked like he had gone out to a meeting, and someone shot him and walked away."

He nodded.

She thought about it for several moments. "Was the bullet that killed him shot directly at him or at an angle?"

She was being analytical. Good. "Straight at him. We think someone was probably sitting next to him, took him by surprise and shot him, and then pulled his hat over his eyes and walked away."

"Why didn't anyone hear the shot?"

"It happened of a morning before the park had filled with people, and the killer must have used a silencer. That would make it premeditated."

"Do you have any idea who did it?"

"We don't know who shot him, but I don't think it was Curtis. I think it was someone more mature and experienced. Curtis is young and excitable. This was too cool and calculated in my mind for him to have done it."

"You're not saying you think it's impossible for him to do such a thing, just that the method is not how he would have done it?"

"Right."

"You may be right, but what about Jeb, the night manager?

He shook his head. "I don't know. My instinct is that those two are small-time."

Her eyes glinted in thought. "I tend to agree with you. So where does that leave us?"

Their gazes locked. In spite of the gravity of the discussion, an arc of awareness passed between them. The widening of her eyes told Kyler that she felt it, too. He grinned, seeking to lighten the atmosphere. "Fishing in a bath tub?"

He should have his head examined. The part of his brain that still worked told him to stay away from her. She was only here to do a job. Then she would leave. But another part of him persisted in wanting to see more of her. It was a new experience for him. He was in deep trouble.

When she pulled her hand away and bounced to her feet, he stood as well. They headed on around the loop that would take them back to the public fountain. When they reached it and walked on to her car, he watched her get in it and drive away.

He had meant to ask her if she would be doing another audit tonight, but it had slipped his mind. He headed back to his duties, but he couldn't stop thinking about her. Janelle. The name was growing on him fast.

When he got back to his apartment, he took a shower. Then he pulled out his cell phone. Janelle had said they were working their way across town. He knew where she had already been. He looked up a list of Baldwin's businesses and saw where the next one south would be.

That evening he drove to a fast food place and picked up a burger and fries. Then he drove on to that Gas & Goods and parked at the corner of the lot. He ate and waited. At seven o'clock he saw Lyle Baldwin arrive and park near the side entrance. Janelle was with him.

Kyler climbed out of his truck and strode toward purposefully them.

Chapter 8

"Mr. Baldwin."

Janelle and Lyle both turned at the voice. She stifled a gasp when she recognized Kyler. Out of uniform, hatless, and wearing jeans and a tee shirt, the sight of him made her stomach flutter. As heat flushed her cheeks, she was glad for the dim lighting in that location.

"May I speak with you for a moment, Mr. Baldwin?" His voice held a note of calm determination.

Lyle studied him in slow detail before responding. "The name's Lyle. Let's go inside where it's private."

His manner gave Janelle the impression that Lyle wasn't particularly surprised at Kyler's appearance. When he unlocked and opened the door, she scuttled inside ahead of them.

Debra rose from the desk and rounded it. "It's all yours. I'll check on you in two or three hours."

Janelle claimed the now vacant desk chair and placed her purse on the floor by her feet. She sneaked a look at Kyler, and caught him doing the same at her. She whisked her attention to the records laid out before her.

"I want to be transparent with you, Mr. ...Lyle," Kyler said, gripping a set of keys tightly in his hand. "I know who Janelle is, and she didn't tell me. I figured it out on my own. Then I pressed her into telling me what you're doing. I had seen you two together and followed you to places where you were working."

Lyle's white topped head moved slowly up and down. He was a tough businessman, and his manner could be brusque to the point of intimidation. But he was known to be fair. "Why did you do that? Did you suspect us of something ...clandestine?"

Janelle glanced up in time to see Kyler's Adam's apple bobbing.

"It was more like confirming, Sir. I'm invested in finding your son's killer, and I couldn't overlook anything that didn't look right."

"Are you telling me this to be sure I don't blame Janelle for anything?"

He swallowed again. "Partly. The other reason is that I don't believe Jordan was doing anything crooked, and I want to help you prove it."

No longer feigning disinterest, Janelle watched Lyle's expression morph from resentment to skepticism, and then to something softer. "Thank you, Winston. I'll talk it over with Janelle, and we'll let you know if we find anything in my accounts that we think points to a murderer."

"How many audits do you have left to do?"

Lyle glanced at Janelle, and then back to Kyler. "This one and the restaurant."

Janelle jumped into the conversation. "I haven't finished with the last one. I only let you think I was done because I want to return to it when Jeb Adams isn't working." She aimed an apologetic look at Lyle.

His heavy brows shot up. "If that's what you want, that's what we'll do. I'll check the work schedule and let you know when he'll be off."

"I want both of you to be careful," Kyler said, his gaze a laser beam on Janelle.

Lyle caught the look. "We will."

"Well, thank you for your time." He turned to leave, but paused at the door and looked back at Janelle. "I'm off duty tomorrow. Would you like to go with me to visit Jordan's wife?"

Lyle visibly bristled. "I can't believe my daughter-in-law is in any way responsible for Jordan's death. She's devastated."

"I'm pleased to hear you speak that way of her," Kyler said. "But I've never interviewed her personally, and I'd like to ask her some questions. You never know what little piece of information could be helpful."

Lyle's rigid posture eased a bit. He rubbed his jaw. "She's a good mother and was a good wife to Jordan, but I see what you mean. She's talked to the police, but maybe another person could ask a different question and learn something new."

He turned to study Janelle. "Having a woman along,

and him not being in uniform, might put Gidget more at ease. I think you should go."

Seeing no way to refuse, Janelle shifted her gaze to Kyler. "Where should I meet you?"

"I'll pick you up at nine in the morning if that's okay."

"If that's what you prefer."

He made a positive jerk of his head and left, hat in hand.

"I'll lock this behind me," Lyle said at the door when Kyler was gone. His meaning was clear. She could exit the room, but no one could enter without a key.

Her privacy insured, Janelle proceeded with her audit. When Lyle and Debra returned later with the usual soda and snack, she leaned back in the chair and kneaded her stiff neck and shoulder muscles.

"Jeb isn't scheduled to work tomorrow night," Lyle reported as they assumed seats for their nightly briefing.

"Let's backtrack then," she said tiredly. "The accounts here look clean at this point. I'll know more when I finish."

"Take as long as you need. Let us know when you're ready to leave." Debra stood, and Lyle accompanied her out of the office.

The next morning, Janelle forced herself out of bed, only half awake after not getting home until four a.m. A hasty cup of coffee and a shower helped.

But when she opened the door in answer to its summons at nine o'clock, she came fully awake. Dressed casually in jeans and a pale blue polo shirt,

Kyler looked relaxed and athletic. His hatless, near black hair was neat and short.

He eyed her tan slacks and mint green shirt. "It looks like you're ready."

She picked up her purse, locked the door, and accompanied him to the white extended cab pickup parked in the driveway behind her car that was in the carport. It was another sunny day, pleasant for a drive.

"In the thirties and forties there were probably as many or more fixed races than square ones," Kyler commented as they rolled into view of Oaklawn Park. "With stricter penalties and drug detection methods, fixed races are almost nonexistent now. I hope Curtis wises up before he ends up with more damage than a split lip and bruised face."

He turned onto a private road and drove another quarter of a mile to a new looking split level home. He parked and shoved the truck door open.

Janelle hopped out and met him in front of the vehicle. "For the record, I don't know the woman Jordan married. Or if Lyle has told her I'm in town."

Kyler nodded and rang the doorbell. Within moments the door was opened by a petite blonde woman with a young child in her arms. She stared at them from a wan face.

Kyler extended a hand. "Good morning, Mrs. Baldwin. I'm Kyler Winston from the park service, and this is Janelle Evans, a childhood friend of your husband's. I'm sorry for your loss. May we come in and ask you a few questions?"

She hesitated for a moment, but then stepped back.

"Come in. I've already talked to the police and don't know what more I can tell you."

The room they entered was comfortable without being ostentatious. Spacious. Soft cream carpeting and tasteful décor.

"Have a seat." She motioned at the blue floral sofa and perched on a chair, the romper clad little boy in her lap.

"What's his name?" Janelle asked, her heart going out to the now fatherless child.

The newly widowed woman stroked the boy's hair, sadness darkening her eyes. "This is Eric. He's twenty months old."

"He's a handsome lad. I can see Jordan in him."

Her chin trembling, she looked up. "Thank you. I've heard Jordan and his parents speak of you a few times. You were the little neighborhood girl who played with him and his sister. Jordan said his dad counted on your dad a lot, and he and Michelle cried for weeks after your mother moved away with you and your brother."

Janelle smiled weakly and swallowed hard. "Brodie and I cried as well. I never forgot the Baldwins."

"Did Jordan have any enemies?" Kyler asked, taking over during the emotional moment.

"None that I know of." Her response was soft.

"What about his relationships at work? Were there conflicts with any of his co-workers, anything that he might have mentioned to you that the police don't know about?"

Her head moved back and forth. "Everything was fine so far as I knew. The police have asked me every question I can imagine."

"What about money? Were you under any kind of financial pressure?"

Again she shook her head. "We both had good jobs with decent salaries. He shouldn't have felt pressured. Although …"

"Although what?" Janelle scooted forward to study the woman's expression when she hesitated.

Gidget bit her lip. "Well, he had seemed troubled for a few days, but when I asked what was bothering him, he assured me everything was okay."

"Is there anyone aside from you who would benefit from his death?" Kyler asked.

"Both our employers provide health insurance, and we have life insurance policies, but nothing over the top."

"What about personal relationships? Was there tension with anyone?"

She continued to stroke the little boy's hair and neck. "We have a circle of friends, and we've never had any bad experiences with any of them."

"One of those couples moved away rather suddenly. Can you tell me why?"

She went still, frowning. "You mean the junior high principal and his wife, don't you?"

"Yes."

She drew a deep breath, her gaze darting around the room. "Steve said he had to be near his parents, that his dad has leukemia."

"But you think there was a reason in addition to that, don't you?"

She stared at him, and then her gaze wavered. "I'm not sure."

"If you're avoiding telling me he's a heavy gambler, don't bother. I've already learned that much about him."

She heaved what seemed to Janelle a sigh of relief. "I'm worried about them," she admitted. "I'm afraid Steve's running from creditors. But I don't believe he would hurt Jordan. He had no reason."

Janelle nodded. "You get along well with Jordan's parents, don't you?"

Her expression lightened. "Oh, yes. They've been wonderful to me. Lyle even gave my brother Spencer a job while he was in college. He's out now, but he still works for them. Lyle made him manager of one of his businesses."

Janelle welcomed the positive vibes she was getting. "Has your brother ever indicated any problems at work?"

Gidget turned thoughtful, pulling the restless tot to her chest and patting him on the back. "He's always seemed happy with his job, and is planning to marry soon, but now that you mention it, he said something recently that made me wonder if things aren't going so well. Something about another worker had him not very happy. I can't remember why, though."

Janelle spoke up. "Could it have been about the night manager?"

Gidget frowned. Then her head began to move slowly up and down. "I think it was. I don't remember details, but Spencer seemed to think the guy's not very honest, and that he has some questionable friends coming around the business."

The little one began to cry, and she stood, rocking him in her arms.

Janelle glanced at Kyler, and they stood also.

"Thank you, Mrs. Baldwin. You've been very cooperative and helpful. If you think of anything else, however small, don't hesitate to contact one of us."

After leaving the house, they headed back to town, and reviewed what they had learned as they rolled north.

"I don't think she has any idea who killed her husband," Janelle said, feeling unexpectedly protective of the woman.

"I don't either," he agreed. "Did you find anything odd in your audit last night?"

"No, but tonight I'm going back for a second look at the one with discrepancies. Lyle told me later last night that Jeb isn't on duty tonight."

He glanced at his watch. "It's only ten o'clock. Do you have anything else on your schedule today?"

She tipped her head sideways. "No, but it sounds like you have something in mind."

He glanced over and grinned, then returned his focus to the highway. "I'm sure you know the Hot Springs history of wide open prostitution and gambling from 1927 until 1967, but I'm guessing you've never visited the gangster museum that was established only a few years ago. Would you like to stop in for a look at the city's colorful past, and maybe go to lunch together?"

"That sounds like fun."

~

Kyler wanted to take Janelle's hand as they walked down the street from where he had parked, but he opted to not push his luck. Having her agree to come had to be enough for now.

He had been in the museum several times, but it was fun bringing newcomers, and even better that Janelle was his companion today.

The workers wore fedoras and pinstripes and spoke with what was supposed to be gangster accents. The first thing their guide explained was that Hot Springs had always been neutral territory, a place where hoods vacationed. There had been an unwritten rule that when mobsters were there, everyone left their battles behind. Gambling was technically illegal, but done in public without fear of retribution. Free-flowing booze, prostitutes, and half a dozen major casinos made the town a bigger gambling destination than Las Vegas.

Three of the biggest gangsters of all time were showcased: Al Capone, Lucky Luciano, and Owen Vincent Madden. A separate gallery was dedicated to each one, featuring photographs, news clippings, and artifacts depicting their lives, including Al Capone's original 1928 Cadillac.

Janelle seemed caught up in the history of the era, judging by the way she examined the slot machines, gaming tables, and weapons. But she said very little.

When they walked back out onto the street, she inhaled deeply and gazed around, feeling nostalgic. "When I lived here I was too young to grasp the history of the town. Now I can imagine how it was back then. I'm sure there must have been a division of local reactions when the Arkansas State Police shut the doors on the last of the illegal casinos."

"I'm sure you're right."

"I'm always right," she boasted, grinning. "I'm a woman."

Yes, she was a woman—a beautiful one. He took her hand and led her to his truck.

When they were inside, he started the motor and pulled into traffic. "Do you have a preference for lunch?"

"Do you know where to find some good Mexican food?"

"You bet."

The meal passed all too quickly, and he had to take her home. Back at her house, he parked and shut off the motor. Then he turned to face her. "Thank you for going with me. I enjoyed having you along."

She faced him, and their eyes locked. "Thank you for including me."

He should get out of the truck. He knew that. But a form of inertia kept him in place. His gaze traveled over her features, taking in each detail, and lingered on her mouth.

The air shimmered with charged awareness. The scent of her perfume and shampoo teased his senses, making him breathe deeper.

He wanted nothing more than to kiss her.

Chapter 9

Janelle's heart thudded against her chest wall. Her pulse raced. Scrambled thoughts tumbled through her mind. She hadn't known Kyler long enough to have this insane wish for him to kiss her. There was no place for this relationship—or whatever it was—to go.

As he moved closer, she swayed toward him. And when he traced his fingertip along the line of her jaw, she didn't pull away. When she lifted her face, he bent his head and kissed her tenderly. Janelle's heart turned handsprings. As his lips moved over hers, she returned the caress.

After a long, sweet moment, he pulled away, a smile on his lips, and gently cupped her cheek. "I don't really want to leave you. I'm feeling things I've never felt before."

"It felt right," she said, scooting to the door. "But it's not practical."

Afraid of what was happening to her, Janelle walked with Kyler to her door and unlocked it without looking at him. Only when she was inside the entry did she do that. "Let me know if you learn anything new."

She closed the door.

That evening Lyle picked her up and delivered her at the usual time. She set to work promptly. Already familiar with the account, she began examining receivables and payables more carefully. It was near midnight when she recognized that the amount of the monthly payment to an account by the name of Worldwide Supply equaled the total of the extra weekly deposits.

"Gotcha!" She pumped a fist in the air, a thrill of elation racing through her.

As soon as her heart rate settled down, she began checking back records. And, sure enough, there was a pattern.

Jan leaned back in the chair, going over facts and figures in her mind. She knew that launderers sometimes placed dirty money in shell companies, fake ones created for the sole purpose of cleaning it. Those companies took money as payment for supposed goods, but actually provided no goods or services. They simply created the appearance of legitimate transactions through fake invoices and balance sheets.

The arrival of Lyle and Debra was timely. "I've found where the extra money is going. Here's a copy of an invoice with an address and contact numbers." She pushed the paper across the desk to Lyle. Then she outlined to them what she had learned.

He studied the invoice, his expression grim. "I'll check out this company tomorrow."

Janelle shook her head. "I think you should let the police do that. I'm not even sure you should check the items on the invoices against your inventory, and risk alerting those responsible that we're onto them."

Lyle eyed her across the desk. "I'm not sure I agree with you, but I'll trust your judgment. Are you finished for the night?"

"I'd like to type up a report of my findings." She tapped a fingernail on the desktop. "I'm wondering if we should wait until we've finished our cycle of audits before going to the police."

Debra stepped over next to her husband. "I think that makes sense. The more information we have to offer them, the faster they can move."

Lyle's expression said he still didn't agree, but he swallowed his impatience. "You're doing good work, so I'll let you carry on as you see fit. Since that's why I asked you to come," he added in wry concession.

After Janelle crawled into bed that night, she lay there staring up into the darkness, anger and helplessness rolling inside her. Were bank officials as diligent about watching for suspicious transactions as they should be? Did they suspect anything? She wanted to visit the bank again, but she had already made herself conspicuous. Yet she felt compelled to meet more of the personnel, someone higher up the chain of command. What excuse could she use?

The next morning she slept late, but once she was up, dressed, and had eaten a bowl of cereal, she drove to the bank. She crossed the lobby to the reception desk, reaching deep inside her for a boldness she didn't feel. The young woman who had occupied it on Janelle's previous visits was not there. Good. "I'd like to speak to the bank president, please."

"May I ask your name and the nature of your visit?" the buxom, older brunette asked.

"I'm Jan Blevins, and I want to ask for guidance about opening a business account."

The woman pushed a button on the intercom. "Mr. Billings, a lady would like to speak with you about a business account." She paused. "Okay."

She disconnected and looked back at Janelle. "He can see you now. It's the first office there." She pointed to the other side of the lobby.

Janelle thanked her and headed that way. As she approached the door, it was opened by a man who was older than the officers she had met previously.

"Come in, Miss Blevins. Do you want to open a business account with us?"

She took the seat he indicated while he returned to his desk. "I'm not sure. I don't have an LLC license or state sales tax number yet, but I'm working on it."

He nodded. "That sounds good. Are you running into problems?"

"No, but I'm concerned about how to avoid my financial transactions being flagged for suspicious activity," she said, sure by now that she was making an idiot of herself. "I know banks train their tellers and account representatives in anti-money laundering."

His brows furrowed. "I think your concerns are

unnecessary, but if it'll put your mind at ease, I can tell you that you'll need to be cautious about showing any sudden, large increase in funds or overly large withdrawals. Will you be moving money to countries hostile to the United States?"

"No, but I figure foreknowledge about those matters will help me avoid mistakes. Someone gave me the impression that you watch closely for laundering operations. Are those a major problem?" She watched his face closely, but detected no reaction.

His smile faded, though. "I assure you we monitor our accounts closely. We know the identity of our customers, and understand the sort of transactions in which they're likely to engage."

Oh, yeah? You don't know me.

"If that's all you need, I really am a busy man." He directed a meaningful glance at the clock on the wall.

Janelle had hoped to accomplish more. Make that something. Anything. But this had obviously been a bad idea. She stood. "Thank you for your time."

Back in her car, Janelle felt a little silly for this wild goose chase that had netted her nothing but a big fat goose egg.

As she drove home, her mental wheels clicked along apace with the wheels of her car, not sure how to connect anything directly to Jordan's murder. All she had was an uneasy feeling about his co-workers in general. She fumed in frustration.

Help me, Lord. Give me direction.

She drew a deep breath and exhaled slowly. God was in charge. She had to trust Him to provide answers.

Her brain refused to shut down. When she entered the house, she pulled the folded newspaper from her oversized purse and settled on the sofa to reread the article about Jordan's death. When she finished, she was no wiser.

She stretched out on the sofa and closed her eyes. The image of the park and that bench floated into her mental vision. Then came memories of her first trip there. A wheelchair rolled down the street, veered across the lawn, and crashed into a tree. Then, within moments, a cop was conveniently there to arrest the driver and issue a ticket.

Was it normal for that officer to be in that area at that time of day? It had been almost the same time of day that Jordan had been killed.

She rubbed her eyes and bolted upright.

~

Kyler paused on his way into the ranger station and checked his ringing cell phone. He was pleasantly surprised to see Janelle's ID.

He answered with a cheerful, "Hello, Miss bench sitter. Are you already missing me?"

She snickered. "I'm missing your input. Do you have time to meet and answer another question or two for me?"

"I've just returned from lunch and have a bit of paperwork to do. I can meet you in thirty minutes in front of the Buckstaff."

"I'll be there." The line went silent.

As Kyler took care of his paperwork and then walked

to the steps of the Buckstaff, thoughts of Curtis continued to nag at him. He pitied the guy for his gambling addiction, if that was his problem. But he couldn't overlook it if he was involved in anything criminal. He thought of a way Janelle could help him learn more about the young man, if she would.

He stopped at the top of the steps and turned to see her marching toward him like a woman with a purpose, which he knew by now that she was.

"I'm not sure I should have bothered you," she said as she climbed the steps to join him.

"You're no bother. But there's clearly something bothering you. Let's go inside where it's cool and see if we can remedy that."

He nodded at Henry behind the desk as he steered Janelle to a seat in the corner of the lobby. When they were seated, he faced her. "What is it?"

She grimaced, her expression troubled. "It's probably nothing. But after rereading the news article about Jordan, I started thinking back over everything, including the day we met." She flushed a bit, giving him hope that their meeting had been as meaningful to her as it had been to him.

He grinned. "You witnessed a crash."

She nodded. "That had just happened, but a cop appeared immediately. I'm probably paranoid, but how did he get there so fast?"

Kyler tipped his head, his expression reflective. "Ivan works this area regularly, just as other officers do."

Her mouth moved in a thoughtful twist.

"Say what's on your mind."

She glanced around. "Was he on duty in that area when Jordan was killed?"

Kyler thought back. "A tourist found him and called nine-one-one. I think Ivan was the first officer on the scene."

She pressed her lips together. "I don't understand how Jordan could have been shot and left in a busy place like that without someone noticing something. Even with a silencer, wouldn't there have been *some* sound?"

Unease made his shoulders itch. That silencer had always bothered him. "Movies make us believe that a silencer mutes gunfire to a whisper, but what it actually does is make a large gun sound like a small gun. There should have been some sound. And someone should have heard it. The tourist said she heard nothing. She just saw Jordan sitting there like he was asleep. But then she noticed blood running down his chest and called the police."

Janelle sat quietly, introspectively.

"I wasn't on duty that morning, and I don't know what police officer was assigned to the area, or what difference it makes, but I'll see if I can find out."

"Thank you. I agree that it probably doesn't make a difference, but it won't hurt to know."

"Wait," he said, placing a hand on her arm when she started to stand. Then he grinned. "Do you need a bath?"

Her mouth dropped open. "Do you think I need one?"

He chuckled. "Yep. While indulging in a traditional thermal bath you might be able to get an attendant or other employees to talk to you about Curtis."

Chapter 10

Janelle watched a smile play around the corners of his mouth. Then she considered the prospect of finding out something—anything—about Jordan's possible killer. "I think I do feel an urge to get wet. As a kid, I used to love coming to the park with my family, and I wondered about what went on inside these places. But I never found out."

He placed a hand on her arm and steered her toward the front desk. "Hey, Henry. This is my friend Jan. She wants a bath."

The big man flashed a wide smile. "Does she want the package or just the bath?" He directed his next words at her. "The massage takes another twenty minutes and costs extra."

She shrugged. "Give me the works. I might never do this again."

"Sure thing." He rang up the charge.

She reached into her purse for her wallet.

"No, you don't. I want to give you a bath," Kyler insisted, amusement glinting from his eyes.

She wasn't about to touch that line.

"He can afford it, Ma'am," Henry said with a chuckle, reaching for the credit card Kyler handed him.

Janelle replaced her wallet. "This is my gig. I should pay."

"You're rendering services I couldn't have managed," he insisted.

"Would you like to deposit your purse and valuables for safekeeping here at the desk?" Henry asked.

As she handed him her purse and watch, a white clad older woman came to meet them, apparently summoned by Henry. "Hello, I'm Roxie," she greeted Janelle pleasantly. "Hi, Kyler. Nice to see you. I promise to bring her back to you all clean and rejuvenated. The men's department is down here," she said to Janelle without a break in her speech. "The second floor is for our ladies. Come with me."

"I'll meet you back here in an hour," Kyler said as she went with Roxie.

"All supplies and linens are provided," Roxie explained as they walked up the hallway.

"Okay," Janelle called back to Kyler as she followed the talkative woman.

Upstairs she found herself looking at a long row of bathing stalls that housed oversized tubs. Shower curtains hung from a rod that spanned the length of them.

"Former presidents, gangsters, celebrities, and

major league baseball players have come here over the years for these baths," Roxie said as she pushed the curtain open on one of the stalls and entered it. "The routine hasn't changed a whole lot. There are lockers for your clothes. Step in here and strip down completely. Don't be modest. I've been doing this for nigh onto twenty years, so nothing bothers me. I'll be back in a jiffy."

Janelle had hardly gotten her shoes off when Roxie returned. She carried a cup of liquid and had a sheet draped over her left arm. "Drink this pure mineral water to prepare your body for the hundred degree bath. Here's a bath sheet to wrap yourself in between processes," she added as Janelle took the cup. She bustled around the end of the tub and began to run water into it.

Janelle drained the cup. "I met a young man at a gas mart who said he works here," she said while unbuttoning her lavender shirt. "He said his name is Curtis Sidebottom."

Roxie glanced up from her stooped position. "Yeah, he's been here a couple of years or so. But I heard he's thinking about quitting."

Janelle frowned, draping the shirt over a chair. "Oh? I got the impression he likes his job."

Roxie stood upright and glanced around conspiratorially. "Just between you and me, I think he's in trouble. I don't know what, but it's something that's getting his face smashed."

"That's too bad." Janelle added her slacks to the chair.

"The tub has its own whirlpool you can use if you want. I'll put these in the locker for you." She picked up the clothes and waited for Janelle to hand her the undergarments.

"You climb in that tub now," she said over her shoulder as she tucked the clothing away. "The bath will be twenty minutes, but I'll check in on you to be sure you're comfortable."

When the woman left, Janelle got in the tub and leaned back. As the heat crept through her body, beads of sweat formed on her forehead. As she gradually adjusted, she turned on the whirlpool and closed her eyes. All she had achieved so far was confirmation that Curtis was in some kind of trouble, which in no way connected him to Jordan's death.

At the end of the bath, she wrapped herself in the sheet and let Roxie lead her to another room where she was ordered to lie on a padded table. When hot towels were draped over her back, abdomen and legs, Janelle was too breathless to ask questions. Twenty minutes later she was treated to two minutes in a steam chamber, and then ten minutes in a chair-like sitz tub that focused its therapeutic effects on her lower body, and finally a two minute cool down in a needle shower.

The Swedish massage that followed left her feeling so relaxed that she had to jog her brain back to the purpose of this indulgence. But her time with Roxie had ended.

"Enjoy the rest of your day," Roxie said, ushering her from the room.

When Janelle reached the first floor and started up the hallway, she met a young attendant with a bruised face. She glanced at his name badge and read the name Curtis on it.

"Why, hello," she said perkily, scooting to a halt. "You must be the Curtis that a friend told me about. He said I should say 'hi' if I ever came here and saw you."

His eyebrows raised a fraction. "What was the friend's name?"

"Jeb," she said in a flash of inspiration. "Jeb Adams."

Curtis' trained smile remained on his face, but all warmth drained from it. "Who should I tell him I met here?"

She stuck out a hand. "I'm Jan Blevins. I'm new in town. Are you and Jeb natives?"

"Yeah." His expression became guarded, and his gaze darted past her. The vibes coming from him were not those of an attendant welcoming a tourist. Janelle got the feeling he wanted nothing to do with her. "I'll tell him I saw you." He took off down the hall.

Well, that was another dead end. At least she had experienced a pleasant bath. On that thought Janelle headed on to the lobby. When she arrived, she looked around for Kyler, but didn't see him. She reclaimed her purse and watch at the front desk and exited the building. As soon as she reached the first step, she spotted him coming across the grounds. He was not alone.

His companion was a willowy blonde beauty wearing a close fitting designer outfit and high heeled shoes. She dropped something, and Kyler bent to retrieve it. As he returned it, Jan read in his smile and manner that the woman was more than a mere acquaintance. She didn't like the emotion that twanged inside her. She couldn't be jealous. Could she?

At that moment Kyler looked forward and saw her. Her heart did a flip flop when his face broke into a broad smile. As he started toward her, the woman's heels clicked on the path beside him.

"Am I late?" he asked as they met at the bottom of the steps.

"You're right on time," Janelle assured him, glancing at his companion.

He noticed. "Jan, this is Lindsey Anderson, an old friend and classmate. Lindsey, meet Jan Blevins."

Janelle extended a hand. "Pleased to meet you."

"Oh, the same here," Lindsey chirped blithely, clasping Janelle's hand briefly in her salon manicured, polished and ring laden one. She withdrew it to push daintily at a stray lock of hair. "Take good care of Kyler here. He's a very special guy."

The assumption that she and Kyler were a couple made Janelle glance at him. He was grinning.

"At least he was back in high school," Lindsey added.

"That was a long time ago," Kyler said dismissively. Janelle wasn't sure, but she thought she detected a hint of sharpness in his tone.

"Lindsey!" A slender brunette hurried up the path toward them. "Sorry I'm late meeting you," she said breathlessly as she reached them.

"We have plenty of time before the meeting starts." Lindsey smiled at Kyler. "It was good to see you again. Look me up any time you're in Little Rock." With a wave she was gone.

"She's a lovely friend," Janelle said as the two women moved beyond hearing range.

"She's a piece of my past, nothing more," he said easily. "When we were in high school she was pretty, flighty, and not at the top of the honor roll."

"But you dated her," she said, guessing.

He shrugged. "I had a lot to learn. She was the type all the guys pursued, so it was flattering when she pursued me. Before I knew what was happening, she was wearing my letter jacket and class ring." He turned and indicated with a head motion that they should start walking toward the street.

"What happened?" she asked as they strolled along the path.

"It didn't take long for me to discover that she was rather shallow, and that I wanted more from a relationship than there was between us." He grinned over at Janelle. "I couldn't seem to find a girl with both beauty and brains."

Her curiosity was piqued. "How did you get out of the relationship?"

A sheepish look crossed his face. "I'm afraid I played dirty. I had a friend pursue her, and when she agreed to go with him I *accidentally* showed up at the same movie they were attending. When we met in the lobby, I asked for my ring back."

"Did your friend continue to date her?"

Now his eyes glinted. "No way. Mike was too smart to get saddled with a ball and chain he didn't want."

"Did Lindsey ever marry?"

"A couple of times. She divorced the first one, and the second one died. And, in case you're wondering, I admit she's made some recent overtures to me. But I'm not interested. How about you? Have you ever been married or engaged?"

Jan blinked, taken off guard at the sudden reversal of focus onto her. "Nope. No one ever held my interest enough to consider marriage. I wanted to get my degree and start my own business. And accountants aren't exactly known for being social butterflies."

He directed a measuring look over her and halted next to her car. "You have the looks, just not the interest."

She ignored the comment. "I didn't learn anything useful from the attendant upstairs, but I ran into Curtis himself on my way back to the lobby."

His expression became grave. "How did that go?"

She shook her head. "I greeted him and told him I had met a friend of his. He was cordial enough, but when I mentioned Jeb's name, he was definitely nervous. Other than that, I learned nothing."

She pressed the button on her key chain. When the car door lock clicked, Kyler stepped back. "Well, thanks for trying."

~

Watching Janelle drive away, Kyler was disappointed at her lack of success gaining information about Curtis. That avenue seemed hopeless. But then he thought about her saying that Curtis had acted uneasy at mention of Jeb. Could pushing his buttons make the young man more forthcoming? He whipped around and strode back inside the Buckstaff.

"Henry, can you check the schedule and tell me what time Curtis gets off work?"

Henry eyed him across the desk. "I don't have to check. I know his shift. He's off at three. And he'll most likely leave through that door." He pointed at the end of the hall.

"Thanks."

Kyler went about his duties, patrolling the park, conducting a couple of guided tours, providing customer service, answering questions, and helping guests. When he finished an outdoor tour at two-forty-five, he moved to the area near the exit Henry said Curtis would use.

When he saw the young man exit, he angled across the lawn and followed Curtis to his car. Before the young man could get the door open, Kyler stepped up close to him.

"I hear your knife is for hire." He was bluffing, but it got a reaction. Curtis spun around, a wide eyed look of panic on his face, and swung a fist.

Kyler ducked, but the blow glanced off his jaw. He grabbed an arm. "That was quite a number you did on that lady's car. Why did you do it?"

Curtis seemed to wilt before his eyes. But then his mouth clamped shut.

"Okay, let's go down and talk to the Chief of Police

about assaulting an officer."

Curtis remained silent at the police station, even while Kyler stated the assault charge. "I suspect he's involved in Baldwin's murder," he said to Ben after a deputy took Curtis to a cell. "I'm not convinced he did it, but I think he may know who did."

Ben nodded. "I'll have a serious talk with him and let you know how it went."

Kyler started to leave, but remembered something else. "Who from your department was on duty in that area when Jordan Baldwin was killed?"

Surprise registered on Ben's face at the question. "I think it was Ivan, but I'll check."

Kyler waited while he turned to his computer, opened a file and studied it, and then looked back at him. "It was Ivan. What's bothering you?"

"I'm not sure. It just seems he should have been on the scene sooner, or the one to find the body."

Ben seemed taken aback by the idea of raising questions about one of his officers. "He would have been cruising the streets. Surely you aren't thinking he had anything to do with the man's death."

"Oh, no," Kyler said quickly. "I'm just trying to get a clearer mental picture of what must have happened, and it seems to me that the murder went undetected for longer than I would have thought possible. Someone had to have left there in a big hurry. It seems that, following the noise of a muffled gunshot, it should have drawn attention."

Ben nodded slowly, skeptically. "I understand. I'll have a chat with Ivan, see if he can shed any light on the picture, or remember why he was so late getting there."

"Thanks. I'd better get back to the park."

An hour later, his cell phone rang. ID said it was Ben. "Yeah."

"We interrogated Mr. Sidebottom. He finally admitted slashing Miss Blevins' tires, but I don't think he had anything to do with Baldwin's murder."

"So why did he slash her tires?"

"He says someone called and told him to do it, and that there would be five hundred dollars waiting for him in a locker at the gym. Curtis said he was scared and didn't want to do it, but he was desperate for the money."

Kyler thought he might know who had made that call, but he wasn't ready to verbalize that to the chief just yet.

Chapter 11

As the week progressed, Janelle continued to work nights in Lyle's businesses. When she finished the last audit, she had no reports of discrepancies in any locations but the one where Jeb Adams worked.

"I'll bring the police in on it now," Lyle said when she gave him her final report. He and Debra sat across from her at a table in the back of his restaurant.

"Thank you for how hard you've worked," Debra said, wiping her mouth with a napkin. "We still don't know who killed our son, but you've done all we asked, and more. How soon do you plan to go home?"

Janelle picked up her purse. "Thank you for the lunch. You've been wonderful to me. I only wish we could have reconnected under better circumstances. I think I'll stick around another day or two and see how things turn out, whether your report leads the police to any answers."

She left them with reluctance, but didn't go straight back to the little house. Instead, she drove to the park, hoping to find Kyler. It was hot outside, and the June sun was still rising.

When she didn't see him on the grounds, and didn't find him at the Buckstaff or the visitor center, she made her way back to her park bench. She gazed across the street where residents and tourists bustled about. Then her eyes rotated to the bathhouses.

The impressive sight made her grin at the thought that the first bathhouses had been little more than brush huts and log cabins built over excavations cut in the rocks to receive hot water that flowed from the Sulphur springs. Unlike most Sulphur water, the water here was pure tasting and odorless.

Her introspection was interrupted by Kyler scooting onto the bench next to her. "Funny finding you here," he said with a mischievous grin.

She shrugged, her heart thumping. "It's a good view. When I didn't find you anywhere else, I automatically returned to my spot."

His brows shot up. "You were looking for me?"

She nodded. "I wanted to tell you that I've finished Lyle's audits, and he's on his way to the police station right now to tell them what we believe one of his night managers is doing."

"Thanks for telling me. I feel like we're close to knowing who killed your friend, but it's still illusive. I've learned only one thing of interest since we last talked."

Her interest piqued. "Spit it out."

He grinned at her sassy order. Then he sobered. "I

asked the police chief about Ivan. He *was* on duty the morning of the killing, and was the first officer on the scene, but he was slow getting there. Something tells me he was nearby and either heard the shot or saw someone leaving."

"But it's just your instincts growling, right?"

His mouth formed a tense line. "Right. I have no proof of anything. I just think Ivan knows something, or at least suspects it."

His phone rang. "Yeah. Be right there." He disconnected and gave Janelle a look of regret. "Gotta go."

~

Kyler hustled to the visitor center where an elderly tourist had fainted. After rendering first aid and summoning an ambulance to take the man and his wife to the hospital, he headed to the ranger station to do the paperwork. As he emerged from the truck, his phone rang. It was the Chief of Police. "Yeah, Ben."

"With the help of an audit report from Lyle Baldwin," he began without preliminaries, "we've arrested Jeb Adams and charged him and Curtis Sidebottom with laundering money for a gambling operation. They haven't coughed up the name of their boss yet, but I think Curtis is about ready to break."

Kyler's grip tightened on the phone. "Thanks for the heads up. Keep after those two."

He made quick work of his paperwork, thoughts and scenes playing through his mind all the while. As soon as he finished, he turned from the computer to stare out the window, unable to escape the questions filtering through his brain about Ivan.

He glanced at his watch. It was time to go off duty. And time to face Ivan. He grabbed his hat, checked out, and went to his personal truck. He knew the general area where the cop should be if he was on duty. He cruised the streets until he spotted a patrol car parked at the curb near the hospital. Ivan sat behind the wheel.

Kyler parked at the first empty space he found and hiked back to the police car. The windows were down, so he opened the passenger door and slid onto the seat.

Ivan's head whirled around. When he recognized Kyler, his expression became guarded. "Is there something I can do for you?" His tone was curt.

"You can tell me where you were parked or patrolling when Jordan Baldwin was killed."

The man's face went red, and he glared at Kyler. "What right do you have to question me?" he huffed.

Kyler struggled for control. "Look, Ivan, I don't like doing it. But I need you to make me understand better what happened. If you were anywhere near where your work schedule says you would likely have been, why didn't you see or hear something sooner?"

He waited for an explanation.

Ivan's jaw worked back and forth. "I think I stopped in at the café down the street for a cup of coffee. As soon as I heard commotion in the street, I ran to the scene."

"Do you have any idea who killed Baldwin?"

Ivan shook his head in quick jerks. "I don't have a

clue."

Without another word Kyler exited the car and headed down the street, feeling the stab of Ivan's stare between his shoulder blades. He walked up to the counter where Mitzi Rogers, the owner, was wiping it with a dish cloth. She looked up. "Hello, Kyler. What can I get you?"

"An answer to a question." He slid onto a stool.

She studied his expression and leaned toward him. "I didn't poison any customers, if that's what's worrying you," she whispered mockingly.

He snorted slightly, and then spoke quietly into her ear. "Were you here the morning Jordan Baldwin was killed?"

Her smile disappeared. "Of course I was. I'm always here."

"Was Officer Young in here at the time?"

She frowned, taken aback, but recovered quickly. She glanced around, as if ensuring no one would overhear. Then she leaned closer. "No, he wasn't. I remember because when I heard the racket outside, I wondered why the dickens there's never a cop handy when needed."

Kyler's gut twisted. "Thanks, Mitzi."

He headed back up the street, just in time to see Ivan's car roll into traffic. Angry at being lied to, and having the liar evade him, he strode to his truck and climbed into it. Hurriedly he started the motor and drove the way Ivan had gone.

It took a few minutes, but he finally spotted the patrol car. He followed at a distance until Ivan pulled to a stop near the park. Kyler parked down the block and practically ran to the patrol car. He tapped on the window next to Ivan. The car motor was still running, the windows up so he could benefit from the air conditioning.

Ivan scowled and lowered the window. "I'm busy. Go on about your own business and leave me alone."

"Not until you tell me the truth. Are you going to talk to me, or are we going to have this discussion at the station with your chief?"

Ivan's eyes closed, and then a look of utter resignation clouded his face. "Get inside," he growled. The window whirred upward between them.

Kyler rounded the car and scooted onto the passenger seat. He looked over at Ivan. "I don't think you murdered Jordan Baldwin, but I think you know who did. You're covering for someone, and I don't understand how you could do that."

Ivan brushed a hand across his eyes, and then rubbed them. Finally, he looked up. A film glistened in his eyes.

"Why?" Kyler breathed forcefully.

"I owed him," the man choked past quivering lips. "We were pals growing up and share a lot of secrets."

"What kind of secrets?"

He stared up through the windshield for several long moments. Then he took a deep breath. "When we were about fourteen, on one of our fishing trips we decided to build a campfire and cook some fish. It was summer and hadn't rained for a while. We went back to the creek to catch another fish and forgot about the

Chapter 12

As the summer crept by, Kyler saw Lyle Baldwin on occasion, sometimes by chance, and sometimes by design. He ate at the man's restaurant far more often than in the past, and stopped by his corporate office now and then on the pretense of giving or receiving updates on the case against Crenshaw and his underlings.

"Hello, Kyler." Lyle slid onto the chair across the table from him. "It's been nice seeing you around more. I hear that Officer Young has been suspended from his job and is facing charges."

Kyler's mouth formed a grim line. "Yes. I understand how he felt about his friend, but there are mandatory reporting rules for people in positions such as his. I hope I'm never put in any kind of situation like that."

Creases appeared between Lyle's eyebrows. He tipped his head. "I get the feeling you would do the right thing—unless a certain gal was involved. Don't bother to deny that you're missing her and hungry for any tidbits of information you can glean from me about her." He smirked.

Kyler felt heat creeping up his neck, but he didn't bother to deny it. "Have you heard from her lately?"

Lyle leaned back in his chair, arms folded across his chest. He chuckled. "From all reports, she's doing fine. But I think she's fighting the same affliction as you."

"Affliction?"

Now the man laughed outright. "Yep. I think you're each so sickly besotted with the other that you can't think straight."

Kyler studied the older man's smug expression. "You really think so?"

He nodded. "Yep."

Kyler snorted. "So you think you're a doctor, huh?"

"In this case I am."

The man was having way too much fun nettling him. And he wasn't done.

"I have a prescription for your malady."

Kyler raised his brows. "Oh?"

"Marry the gal."

The very idea had been floating around in his head, but he didn't know how to go about it—or have the courage.

Suddenly Lyle's expression went sober, and he leaned forward on his arms on the table. "Do you love her enough to move to Indiana?"

Kyler didn't respond, but his face must have revealed his answer.

Lyle grinned. "Before you go filling out job applications, find out if she's willing to move here. She likes Hot Springs. And I'd love having her around."

Kyler scowled. "You've reached the point of meddling now, friend."

Lyle's grin was unrepentant, but he pushed to his feet. Before walking away, he paused. "One more thing."

Kyler waited, wary.

"She has a birthday next week."

~

The month of June had been long. As the calendar rolled into July and the weather grew ever hotter, Janelle tucked the memory of Kyler's kiss deep inside her and buried herself in work. Her assistant had done a good job in her absence, but there were things she had to do personally, accounts to check, clients to contact, and a hundred other things.

Her birthday had crept up on her. In some ways she didn't feel twenty-nine. In others she felt older, and empty. She had learned that it was possible to be lonely in the midst of a busy, people-filled life.

"You're wool gathering again."

Terri's comment made Janelle jerk her head around from staring out the window, shaking off her preoccupying thoughts of Kyler.

Terri stood in front of the desk, wearing a Cheshire smile and holding a huge vase of flowers. A balloon floated above them, anchored to an ear of the vase by a string, and proclaiming HAPPY BIRTHDAY.

She set them on Janelle's desk. "I'll get your mail

while you read the card in private." Her tone implied it was from a sweetheart.

Puzzled, but her heart leaping with hope, Janelle opened the card—and nearly wept with joy when she saw the message.

I miss you. Meeting you touched my life and heart in a wonderful way.

It was signed by Kyler.

She was still sitting there in a benumbed state when Terri returned and placed a packet of envelopes and a newspaper next to the vase. "You have a dreamy look on your face. Are you ever going to tell me about him?"

"About him?" Janelle repeated evasively.

Terri snickered. "You haven't been the same since you returned. And now he sends you those." She nodded at the flowers. "Tell me his name."

"Kyler Winston," she said obediently.

"How does he fit into your visit to Hot Springs?"

"He's the park ranger who helped put it all together."

Terri whistled. "I think it's a good thing I was going to be resigning."

That brought Janelle upright in her chair, totally caught by surprise. "You do? You are?"

"My husband has been promoted and transferred to Indianapolis. He has to report to the new job right after Labor Day."

Janelle stared at her assistant's back as she walked away, struggling to absorb this sudden announcement. Then she picked up the envelopes and flipped through them. She was pleasantly surprised to find a letter from Lyle among them.

By the time she'd finished reading it, she was in awe. Only God could have programmed all this. Lyle had written that his latest business acquisition was an office complex, and an office in it was her birthday present and payment for helping solve Jordan's murder, if she wanted it.

As the pieces clicked together in her mind, she reached for the phone to thank Lyle. After the call, she wrote a note to Kyler, thanking him for the flowers and telling him how much she had enjoyed her time getting reacquainted with the Baldwins and Hot Springs, and meeting him.

Within days she closed her business and relocated it to Lyle's office building. Due to the suddenness of the transition, she had moved back into the little house on Ramble Street.

Janelle was in her new office Monday afternoon, removing supplies from boxes and shelving them, when the sound of the door opening made her whirl around. When she saw Kyler enter, her heart thumped into overdrive.

He came to an abrupt halt, a look of utter surprise crossing his face when he recognized her. He glanced around at the clutter of open and unopened boxes on the floor, and the in-progress organization of the room.

Janelle inhaled sharply and released the breath slowly to calm her racing heart. But it didn't work. "Who ...what can I do for you?" she stammered.

He moved on into the room and stopped near her. "Lyle called and said I should come to this address to pick up something that …be …longs …to me."

Her system went into near cardiac arrest at the audacity of what Lyle had done. Then sheer elation shot through her veins that the man knew how deeply she was in love with this handsome ranger.

She swallowed. "I think he was being presumptuous, overstepping the bounds. Please forgive him."

A grin worked its way across Kyler's face, and he stepped over next to her. He placed his hands on her arms and looked directly into her eyes, searching. "I hope he was just being intuitive. He's figured out that I love you and want nothing more than to marry you."

She stepped fully into his embrace, tears of joy stinging her eyes. With his heart thudding in her ears, she wrapped her arms around him and whispered, "I happen to love you, too. So much."

"I thank God for bringing you into my life," he whispered back. "And I want you there forever."

Janelle thought her heart would burst with happiness.

Neither of them noticed Lyle's car drive slowly by in front of the office. Wrapped in one another's arms, they were too occupied with kissing and dreaming of the future.

The End

BOOKS by Helen
MOZARK MARRIAGES
Ozark Sweetheart
Ozark Reunion
Ozark Wedding

DODGE CITY DUOS
Bandit Bride
Prairie Bride
Dodge City Duos (2 in 1: Bandit Bride & Prairie Bride)

HEARTLAND HEARTMATES
Show Me Love
Heartland Illusions
Mozark Vision
Missouri Catch
Heartland Heartmates (4 in 1: above series)

BOOTHEEL BRIDES
Bootheel Bride
Bootheel Bachelor
Bootheel Betrothal
Bootheel Brides (3 in 1: above series)

LAKE OZARK LADIES
Paige's Proposal
Brooke's Bargain
Haley's Hero
Kelsey's Keeper

NOVELLAS by Helen
Hawthorn Hope
Tree of Hope
River Town Romance (2 in 1: Hawthorn Hope & Tree of Hope)
 Pasque Plight
Black-Eyed Susan's Secret
Love Blooms (2 in 1: Pasque Plight & Susan's Secret)
Shamrock Ruby
Dream Team
Mother Road Matches (2 in 1: Shamrock Ruby & Dream Team_

Made in the USA
Las Vegas, NV
03 September 2021